Lorel slapped him as hard as she could

Then she looked at him in horror, her heart pounding. "I—I'm sorry..." she began.

But it was too late. Steve Kennedy's hands shot out, tangling in her hair, dragging her toward him while she struggled, his face tight with rage.

His hard mouth came down on hers, forcing her lips apart. One hand clamped the back of her neck ruthlessly, fiercely, as he deepened the kiss.

Lorel flailed her arms uselessly against his shoulders, tears burning her eyes, as his hard body pressed her against the wall, his mouth inflicting a combination of pain and pleasure.

Then he spoke harshly against her face. "Remember me now, Lorel?"

English writer **SARAH HOLLAND**, after going to school in London, struck out on her own. She worked in various offices around London, and also as a singer in a recording studio, until illness forced her to return to her family, who had moved to the Isle of Man. There she started writing for Harlequin, and while, according to Sara, her first book was not very good, she was encouraged to keep on. Her second book, *Too Hot to Handle*, was accepted immediately, and since then she has had more than five novels published. Though she is interested in theater and has taken a course at a drama school in London, she says she will continue to write romantic novels.

Books by Sarah Holland

HARLEQUIN PRESENTS
516—TOO HOT TO HANDLE
536—TOMORROW BEGAN YESTERDAY
552—THE DEVIL'S MISTRESS
576—DEADLY ANGEL
601—FEVER PITCH

HARLEQUIN ROMANCE
2705—BLUEBEARD'S BRIDE

SARAH HOLLAND

---

the heat is on

Harlequin Books

TORONTO • NEW YORK • LONDON
AMSTERDAM • PARIS • SYDNEY • HAMBURG
STOCKHOLM • ATHENS • TOKYO • MILAN

For Ann Dalton

Harlequin Presents first edition August 1989
ISBN 0-373-11192-4

Original hardcover edition published in 1988
by Mills & Boon Limited

CHAPTER ONE

IT WAS just after midnight and the party was in full swing. Lorel had escaped to the kitchen, needing light and fresh air. The lace curtain fluttered in the breeze, and Lorel leant against the sink, eyes closed. Her red-gold hair was tousled, damp with sweat from dancing. Behind her, Madonna blasted out of the stereo and dancers undulated like rubber snakes in the hot and crowded living-room.

'It's a roaring success!' Mary came in behind her, a whirlwind of blonde hair and blue eyes. 'Even Freddie's impressed!'

'Last time I saw Freddie——' Lorel slid wry green eyes to her flatmate '—he was slowly sliding down a wall!'

'He's just celebrating.' Mary hunted in the fridge for a bottle of wine. 'You know he starts filming that BBC play next week?'

'He told me.' Lorel felt a sigh escape her lips. 'I wish I had half his talent.'

'You have.' Mary looked at her quickly, her face suddenly serious.

Lorel met her frank gaze and smiled. Thank God for Mary! At least she understood. And was always there wherever Lorel's faith in herself wavered. But then, so was Freddie. They all were. All her old friends from Drama School kept her faith constantly buoyant, supporting her even now when she didn't even have a waitressing job any more.

It had been two years since she'd left Drama School. Freddie had just gone from success to success, and even Mary was beginning to pick up good, strong parts now. But all Lorel had to live on at the moment was the possibility of passing a screen test next week with Luchino Piccardi, and that wasn't really very much.

'When's the screen test?' Mary closed the fridge, watching her closely. 'Wednesday?'

Lorel nodded. 'I'm terrified!'

'Nonsense,' Mary said firmly. 'The camera will love you. Look at those bones!'

'Poverty is so good for the figure!' Lorel sighed, looking down at herself. The black taffeta mini-dress showed her slender legs to advantage, her red-gold hair tumbling in fiery disarray on to elegantly boned shoulders.

It was starvation, of course. Nobody was this slim on a healthy diet. But she had lost her job waitressing at Covent Garden a month ago, and jobs were scarce in London. Her savings were running low and she didn't dare ask her parents for help. They would tell her to come home, give up the stage. This screen test looked like her last change.

'Just remember,' Mary wagged a slim finger at her, 'don't act. Be yourself and behave naturally . . .' she broke off as there was a sudden crash from the bathroom, followed by wild shrieks of laughter from the hall.

Lorel put down her drink. 'I'll go.'

Pushing through the crowds of people clustered around the bathroom door, Lorel stumbled into the well-lit room and took in the scene at once.

'Oh, Freddie!'

He was sitting in the bath with a plant pot on his head, earth and leaves sliding slowly over black curly hair, ruining his dark, expensively cut evening suit, his long legs dangling over the edge of the bath like a wooden clown's.

'Sorry about this,' he said with careful deliberation. 'I was checking to see if there was a fire escape. There wasn't. I slipped and found myself in this perfectly lovely bath.' He looked up at her with little-boy brown eyes. 'I'll replace the plant, of course.'

Lorel dimpled and went to his aid. 'You idiot!'

She helped him stand, and he leant on her, his mouth curving in a gypsyish smile as he deliberately made the most of it, one arm around her shoulders, holding her close.

Lurching out of the bath, one long leg at a time, he said suddenly, 'I say! What a great double-act we'd make.'

Lorel gave him a wry look. 'Freddie and Ginger?'

He laughed. 'Absolutely! Hey—that's a brainwave! I think you should do your *Cabaret* routine. That'll liven the party up.'

'No,' Lorel said immediately, because you had to be firm with a man like Freddie. 'Absolutely not.'

'Boo!' Freddie leaned towards her, swaying, his brown eyes narrowed. 'Hiss. Spoilsport.'

She laughed. 'Sticks and stones, Freddie. I had to do that stupid dance routine all the way through Drama School and beyond. There is nothing you could say or do to persuade me to do it now.'

Five minutes later, she found herself locked in the bathroom with Freddie while he leant her his top hat and silver-topped cane to do her *Cabaret* routine with. She was resigned but rather irritated about being railroaded into doing it. All through Drama School she had performed it every time an occasion worthy of a high-kicking dance routine came up. It was fun, and she did enjoy it. But it had certainly not been on the agenda tonight.

'Don't sulk,' Freddie said firmly, adjusting her top hat to the correct angle so that she looked a little like a long-haired Dietrich. 'It makes you look ugly.

'I don't care.' Lorel studied herself in the mirror, seeing the slanting green eyes and pale pink mouth set in a definite sulk. 'You shouldn't have pushed me into this.'

'Why?' His face was seriously suddenly. 'It gave me five minutes alone with you, didn't it?'

Lorel bent her head, not meeting his gaze, and there was a long pause. Uncomfortable, she fiddled with the carved top of the cane, her fingers sliding over it as she felt him watching her intently.

Moistening her lips, she said, 'Stephanie's here.'

His mouth tightened. 'I'm not interested in

Stephanie!'

'She likes you . . .'

'And I am in love with you!' Freddie interrupted flatly, his hands taking her shoulders and turning her to face him, ignoring the hot flush that burnt her cheeks, made her refuse to lift her head and look at him.

They had had this conversation so many times before. What was the point of having it again? He couldn't accept that she only wanted him as a friend. Only needed his friendship, not his love, not like this.

His hand pushed under her chin. 'Who are you waiting for, Lorel? Mr Right? He's not going to show up, you know. You might as well face that, and face it fast!'

Stung, she pulled away and unlocked the bathroom door, her face angry enough to keep him at bay. 'I've been over this too many times with you. What's the point in discussing it again?'

'I'm going to Manchester next week,' Freddie said tonelessly. 'That's the point. I want you to come with me.'

She stared at him, and slowly shook her head. 'What about my audition?'

'After that. Come down after that.' His eyes searched her face eagerly. 'I'm playing in the big league this time, Lori. I'm going to need support.'

She bit her lip, not knowing how to let him down without hurting him or making him feel alienated. 'I can't,' she said huskily. 'You know I can't.'

His mouth tightened and he watched her through

his lashes, making her saddened because every time he pressurised her like this, something between them died.

He turned his back on her, hands in his pockets, his long, lanky body stiff with hurt pride. 'You'd better go in. They're playing your song.' Looking back over one shoulder, he sang bitterly, 'What good is sitting alone in your room . . .?'

Lorel flushed hotly and left the bathroom, closing the door with a quiet click behind her. People were so complicated. If only her relationship with Freddie could have stayed the way it had been at Drama School, with just a strong bond of friendship between them.

Carbaret blasted from the stereo as she entered the living-room, and she felt excitement flood her veins, high-kicking her way in, hat tilted and hips swaying to the music.

'On the table!' shouted someone from the back, and Lorel did as she was bid, her green eyes glittering as she took centre stage, swaying seductively in the half-light, her eyes half closed and her mouth softly parted.

There was a commotion in the hall, hammering on the front door followed by angry words, but Lorel barely heard it, completely lost in the dance now, one hand sliding up the back of her neck to push her red-gold curls into a heavy mass as she turned her back on the audience, looking provocatively over one shoulder.

A man stormed across the room, and the record was switched off suddenly.

Lorel froze, hair tousled and tangled, her eyes slightly dazed as she stared into the darkness, straightening and turning around.

'Who did that?'

'I did,' a deeply drawling voice said.

A man stood in the centre of the room, hands on hips, watching her with heavy-lidded blue eyes, his mouth a hard, uncompromising line, his body tanned and muscular, dressed in a black cashmere sweater and black jeans.

'Who are you?' Mary demanded, stepping forward from the crowd of faces. 'I didn't invite you.'

Lorel felt a frisson of alarm run like ice-cold water down her spine as the stranger slid cool, blue eyes to her as though in reply, and as the silence lengthened, Lorel felt a sudden panic flare in her mind, a panic she fought down immediately, a door in her mind slamming shut.

'Lorel?' Mary was watching her. 'Did you invite him?'

It took a long time for her to answer that. She knew the stranger. Something in her found every line of that hard-boned face desperately familiar, yet she could not place him. Did not *want* to place him.

'No,' she said suddenly, fiercely. 'I've never seen him before in my life.'

The stranger's mouth tightened and she saw a flash of rage in the blue eyes. Then it was gone, and there was only annoyance.

'I'm your upstairs neighbour,' he said flatly.

'My name is Steve Kennedy. And I am not here to enjoy myself! I've been trying to sleep since midnight, and the noise down here has just got worse and worse.'

'We sent out invitations,' Lorel said firmly. 'Didn't you get yours?'

'No,' he said. 'I've been out of the country.'

'I'm sorry.' Lorel looked around at the living-room, the guests all crowding in around her. 'But as you can see, the party is under way now.'

'I don't give a damn,' he drawled tightly, 'I have to be up early in the morning to work, and I don't intend to wear ear plugs all night!'

'We'll try to keep the noise down,' she promised.

His eyes flashed and he stepped towards her, making her senses jump, something pushing at her memory, something so familiar about him that she was almost afraid of him.

'You'll do better than try,' he said under his breath, 'because if I can't get to sleep, I'll come back down, break your records, throw your guests out and call the police.' He leant towards her, his face menacing. 'Now do I make myself clear?'

Her mouth trembled and she heard herself say angrily, 'You can't just break into other people's homes and . . .'

'The door was open,' he said. 'Letting out as much noise as possible. I hammered on it, then pushed it back. What did you expect me to do? Wait politely until you'd finished your act?' His gaze raked her from head to foot and he said bitingly, 'I'm not the Avon lady, darling! And I don't wait for anyone!'

She didn't doubt it. She'd never seen arrogance like this before. He made every hair on the back of her neck prickle.

'That doesn't excuse the fact that you scratched my record!' she said angrily.

'I don't intend to excuse myself,' he said tonelessly. 'Particularly not to a woman like you.' Insolently, he allowed his eyes to rove over her body, taking in the pale shoulders and long legs as he drawled, 'Dancing on the table half-naked for a room full of drunks. This is some party. Maybe I should hang around.' His eyes mocked hers as he added lazily, 'I'm sure you could show me a good time.'

She caught her breath at the insult, eyes furious. 'How dare you? I'm every bit as respectable and hard-working as you are! And so are my guests!'

He laughed, sardonic malice glittering in his eyes. 'Oh, really?'

'Yes!' Indignation made her temper flare. 'And you have no right to judge me!'

'And what do you do for a living?' he drawled. 'Or shall I guess?'

Her face stung and she said tightly, 'I'm an actress.'

'Is that what they call it these days?' he murmured, hard mouth twisting with cynical amusement.

'For your information,' she said under her breath, almost trembling with rage at the sheer contempt with which he watched her, 'I have a starring role in the new Luchino Piccardi film!'

If she'd wanted to wipe that lazy smile off his face she had succeeded. A long silence followed her announcement, a silence which Lorel regretted the minute it fell. He was staring at her, frowning, a dark pair of brows pulling together across his forehead, and Lorel wished she hadn't been quite so impulsive. He wasn't the only one to stare. Her guests were taken aback too, watching her with open-mouthed astonishment, and she prayed silently that they wouldn't give her away.

Steve Kennedy was watching her with narrowed eyes. 'I'm impressed,' he said slowly, thrusting his hands into the pockets of his black jeans. 'What's the name of the picture?'

She lifted her chin with as much dignity as she could muster. *'Eleanor.'*

That lazy smile twisted his mouth again and he said softly, 'Well . . . what do you know . . .!'

Another silence fell between them, and Lorel shifted position, trying to look dignified even though she stood on top of this stupid table in her short dress and top hat, clutching a cane with damp fingers.

'I think you'd better leave,' she said huskily, when he made no move to fire back at her with any more insults.

The blue eyes shot to her face, watching through black lashes, and he smiled, charm changing the dark face as he drawled, 'Sure. I'll go. But remember what I said—keep the noise down or there'll be trouble. Got it?'

She nodded stiffly. 'Got it.'

He turned on his heel and walked out, arrogant stride making *déjà vu* swamp her as she stared after that dark head. He was so familiar. Even the way he walked. The way the dark hair curled thickly at the back of his neck, the lazy grace in that self-assured stride. Where had she seen him before? Why did this *déjà vu* feel so very powerful?

People started talking again as the front door slammed. Groups clustered together, discussing the incident. Someone put soft music on the turntable, cool, lazy jazzy sounds floating out and instantly altering the atmosphere of the party into a quiet and intimate gathering.

Sade sang huskily, about a man who was a smooth operator, and Lorel got down from the table on shaky legs, agreeing with the singer. That was exactly what he was.

'What a nerve!' Mary came up to her, her face tight with anger. 'I've got a good mind to call the police myself!'

'We wouldn't have a leg to stand on.' Lorel shook her head and walked across the floor into the kitchen, needing to think. 'It's way past one o'clock, and we were making a terrible noise.'

'Even so,' Mary followed her, high heels click-clacking on the kitchen linoleum, 'surely the police would tell him off?'

Lorel laughed. 'I don't think that would bother him.'

'You're right.' Mary made a face. 'He's too tough

to be told off.'

Lorel poured herself some orange juice and swallowed it thirstily. She felt thrown off balance, as though something important had happened and she had to find out what it was. How ridiculous! He was a stranger. She'd never seen him before in her life. Then why did she feel this panic? Her hand went to her chest to try to still the sudden fast beating of her heart as Steve Kennedy's face leapt into her mind.

Looking at Mary, she felt a sudden urge to confide. But what could she say? That she was sure she had seen Steve Kennedy somewhere before? That she was scared and she didn't know why? What could Mary possibly say in reply to something as absurd as that? And even if she could come up with some suggestions, how could Lorel shake off this feeling of sudden impending disaster?

Sloane Square glittered under an icy November sun. Cars shot around the tree-lined square, double-parked beneath skeletal branches, clumps of russet-gold autumn leaves lining the gutter and littering the green behind the black iron railings.

Lorel stood on the corner, looking up at the silver logo of Cavalcade Films in the corner of the square, her heart beating with excitement and nerves. This was the biggest break she had ever had. Luchino Piccardi was looking for an unknown to play the part of Eleanor in this film, and it was the chance of a lifetime. She didn't know whether to pray or just trust to luck. If she got the part, most of her problems would be solved. If she didn't—well, she would have to think long and hard.

Ten minutes later, she found herself on the seventh floor in an outer office to Luchino Piccardi's, waiting with around fifteen other red-headed actresses, all of them total unknowns.

Her self-confidence was punctured like a balloon as she looked at them all, knowing full well that her chances were one in a million. They looked back at her with hostile appraisal, fifteen pairs of green eyes sending daggers in her direction. Lorel buried herself in a copy of *Vogue*, pretending interest as she flicked through it with trembling hands.

'Lorelei Lane!'

Her head jerked up and she found herself standing, walking across to the vast oak door with 'Luchino Piccardi' written on it in silver letters.

Taking a deep breath, she knocked on the door and waited, her heart thumping with sickly fear.

'Come in!'

Lorel swallowed, wished herself luck, and pushed open the door.

The door opened on to an office of breathtaking luxury. Green leather armchairs stood on cream carpeting, art deco plant holders in black and silver with palms thrusting out of them like exotic fans. A silver statuette stood in frozen dance on the desk. An Oscar stood opposite it in solemn dignity. Lorel saw the posters on the walls, framed in silver, saw the signed photographs of Hollywood stars, and behind the desk saw Luchino Piccardi himself, relaxed and casual in denim jeans and jacket, a legend with silver hair and a boyish charming smile.

But her eyes flicked past him in sudden shock to the man who was turning away from the window, dressed in black, a rolled-up script in one hand, the other running through his thick black hair.

Steve Kennedy looked at her with cold, mocking eyes, and she was unable to breathe or speak; she just stared at him open-mouthed.

'Why, Miss Lane,' he drawled softly, 'how charming you look today.'

She smiled weakly.

'No top hat?'

This is a nightmare, Lorel thought as she closed the door behind her and stood paralysed where she was. What was he doing here?

'You know each other?' Piccardi said in a lazy Italianate accent.

Steve threw the script on to the table. 'We've met.'

The biting emphasis on the words made her face flame, and she could not meet his eyes. She knew him. Oh God, if she could only remember! Where had she met him? Why did he fill her with this breathless sense of foreboding?

'Sit down, Miss Lane.' Kennedy watched her with narrowed eyes. 'No one's going to bite you.'

Oh, aren't they? Lorel thought, crossing the room on shaky legs and sitting down in a green leather armchair.

Looking up at him through her lashes, she

noticed the wealth and power in every move he made, the arrogant way he stood, the coolly expensive cut of that black suit, the gold watch chain glittering across a tight waistcoat. How could she possibly know him?

His eyes watched her intently. 'Take off your coat.'

It was almost a command to strip, and her fingers fumbled with the belt as she did as she was told, slipping it off and adjusting her green silk dress, aware that those narrowed blue eyes followed every move of her body.

'Now,' he said, 'tell us about your career to date. Have you worked in films before?'

Haltingly, she outlined the bare details of her career, only too well aware that it was not impressive. If only she hadn't been so stupid at the party. Why in God's name had she told him she already had the part in this film?

When she had finished he was silent, watching her with eyes that made her feel vulnerable and under attack. He was going to make sure she didn't get this part. She could see that a mile off. He didn't like her, and he didn't want her in this film. But she had to try! Even though she felt like running out of that office and away from his tight-lipped hostility, she had to try.

'So you're not, in fact, a very experienced actress,' he said coolly, sliding his hand in the pocket of that immaculate black suit. 'Are you, Miss Lane?'

'No,' she said huskily, scarlet colour flooding

her face. 'But I feel I could portray Eleanor. I've read a great deal about her—including all of her own books.'

He smiled, malice in his eyes. 'I want an actress, Miss Lane, not a reader.'

'I am an actress!' Her eyes flashed with resentment. 'Give me a screen test and I'll prove it.'

He laughed. 'Screen tests cost money.' Walking lazily across to where she sat, he perched on the edge of the desk, watching her through thickly lashed eyes. 'How do we know you're worth it?'

'You don't. I'm a risk.'

'Then why should we bother to take you?' His brows rose coolly. 'All I can see on offer is red hair and a sexy body. They're a dime a dozen, Miss Lane. Did you notice that abundance outside?'

'Because that's what your film's all about,' she said carefully. 'Taking risks. Eleanor Browning won against all odds. Isn't that why you want an unknown to play her? Surely a more established actress would detract from the theme?'

He studied her with cool malice. 'I don't think you've got the guts to win against all odds.'

Her eyes flashed with temper and she said tightly, 'If I didn't, I wouldn't be sitting here answering your very hostile questions!'

His brows shot up and he was silent for a moment, watching her.

'She has the face,' Luchino Piccardi spoke lazily, leaning back in his chair and watching her with narrowed eyes. 'Good bones. The temperament, too.'

Lorel held her breath, too shocked by the sudden turn of luck in her favour to move or speak. Her green eyes shot to Piccardi's face, praying he would convince Steve Kennedy to give her a test.

Kennedy looked back at her with a frown. 'You want to test her?'

Lorel did not move a muscle. She wanted to throw a prayer mat on the floor and start desperately trying to win over the gods.

Luchino uncoiled, standing up and walking around her, studying her face from all angles while Lorel sat like a statue, not daring to do or say anything. She was desperately aware of Steve Kennedy's blue eyes burning into her, making her feel off balance, thrown, unconfident. He wanted her to fail. She could feel him willing her to fail.

'Tomorrow morning,' Luchino Piccardi said firmly. 'At nine. Can you get to Cannon-Elstree studios by yourself, or shall we send a car?'

Lorel managed to say breathlessly, 'I'll get there. I have a car.' Why had she said that? She'd always wanted to ride in a studio limousine!

He nodded. 'Fine. Here's your pass . . .' He leant over the desk, scribbled something on a piece of card and handed it to her, not noticing her sweating hands. 'Wear no make-up. We'll get you ready.'

Then she was standing up, her legs shaking, and thanking him in a husky voice, her fingers fumbling for her coat as she belted it tightly at the waist and walked to the door.

Steve Kennedy watched her coolly across the room, blue eyes hooded by those heavy lids and long lashes. 'You're a very lucky girl,' he drawled softly as she met his gaze. 'I'll keep my fingers crossed for you when I watch the test tomorrow.'

She stopped at the door, watching him closely. 'You'll be there?'

'Of course,' he said lazily, 'I wrote the damned thing.'

If anything was calculated to knock her off balance, that was it. For a full minute, she stood in the doorway, staring at him, and felt a growing respect change her view of him as her eyes slid over that hard-boned face. This was the hottest script in the business at the moment. Every one wanted to get hold of it. Established actors were lining up for cameos in it. And Steve Kennedy had written it.

On the way home, she stared out of the grimy train window at London gardens with washing hanging in the back of them, and asked herself more questions than she had ever found spinning in her mind at any other time.

Everything had happened so fast. She felt breathless, light-headed, as though it was really a dream, not actually happening to her. A screen test! With Luchino Piccardi. It was unreal. It was everything she had ever dreamed of.

There was only one blight on the horizon, and that came in the form of Steve Kennedy. He was out to get her, that was a certainty. And she didn't know why. She couldn't arm herself against his relentless attack because she didn't know why it was being directed at her.

He hated her. That was quite clear. He had been grossly insulting at the party, and had tried to shred her confidence into ribbons at the interview today. But why?

Her face flamed scarlet as she stepped out of the train on to an icy platform. She knew why. But she could not tell herself. Her mind was locked tightly shut and she couldn't see in.

It was that feeling of familiarity that was behind his dislike of her, and she knew it. But if only she could understand why. If only she could remember . . .

CHAPTER TWO

AN ICY November mist clung to the roads as she drove down to Elstree next morning. Elizabethan houses clustered on the narrow winding main street, inns beamed and sloping behind an ethereal mist.

At Elstree Studios, she parked, and walked through the security gates, proudly showing her pass as she went on to the busy studio street. Technicians walked past her, scruffy in old jeans and sweatshirts, but with a love of their work on their faces that she understood as they called cheerful greetings to a group of actresses sitting on a step outside a sound stage.

Lorel walked briskly to stage nine and pushed the door open. It swung shut behind her with a hollow thud and people turned to look at her.

'Miss Lane?' A short, dark-haired woman with a clip-board spotted her and came over. 'You're wanted in make-up right away. Down that corridor, first room on the left.'

Lorel nodded, and turned away, grateful to have been organised so soon. Even though she had a right to be there she felt slightly out of place, as though she was an interloper, an outsider. She felt a sudden urge to belong to this busy world, and thanked her lucky stars that Lucino Piccardi had been so good to her yesterday. Without him, she would not be here.

Mary had been delighted, of course, and had leapt all over the flat, wanting to rush out and buy champagne to celebrate with. But of course—it was only a test, and neither of them wanted to tempt fate by celebrating too soon.

Lorel pushed open the door of make-up and walked inside, to find it deserted; a long, low dressing-table with mirror and barely anything else stood at one side, with some chairs around it.

A footstep behind her made her turn, and the blood drained from her face as she saw Steve Kennedy lounging lazily in the doorway, watching her.

'What are you doing here?' she asked huskily, her eyes wary as she stared across the deserted room at him.

He walked in slowly, closed the door and leant on it, his smile alarming her. 'I thought I'd help you with your test. Run through the scene with you.'

'Why should you do that?' she asked stiffly. 'I got the distinct impression yesterday that you hated the sight of me.'

He laughed softly. 'Are you always so paranoid?'

Her mouth tightened. 'I'm not paranoid. I just know when someone doesn't like me!'

'Oh?' he drawled, raising dark brows. 'Women's intuition?'

'That's right.' She struggled to keep her cool, but the knowledge that they were alone together in this room frightened her. 'You've been hostile to me ever since you first set eyes on me.'

'And when was that?' The blue eyes narrowed on her intently. 'When did I first . . . set eyes on you?'

There was a silence. Her mouth went dry. The look in his eyes made her want to run, but she couldn't even speak; her stomach felt suddenly sick and she stared at him, eyes darting nervously, unable to answer the question because her heart was beating with sudden panic.

He straightened, watching her with intense blue eyes, his hands thrust into the pockets of the jeans he wore. 'Well?' the hard mouth said softly. 'Cat got your tongue?'

'I . . .' She swallowed, heart hammering. 'It was the party. You came into my flat. I——'

'I don't think so.' He shook his dark head, white shirt open at the throat to show his tanned skin. 'Try again.'

Panic made her eyes flash angry green. 'That was when we first met!' she said fiercely. 'You know it was!'

The look he gave her as he stopped walking went straight through to the centre of her panic.

'Shall I refresh your memory?' he drawled.

Mute, she shook her head.

He watched her with those ruthless eyes. 'You were eighteen . . .'

'No . . .!'

'Your sister had just got married—to the man you loved. He followed you out into the hotel garden . . .'

Lorel started to tremble, her eyes enormous.

'You told him to go away,' Steve Kennedy continued, his mouth cool and straight as he spoke lazily. 'But he put his arm around you . . . kissed you . . .'

'Shut up!' she hissed, barely able to move or breathe as the memory flooded back, making her go first icy-cold then red-hot with shame.

'I couldn't help overhearing, of course,' Steve drawled, pushing away from the wall and walking with lazy grace across the room. 'I didn't know anyone at the reception. My cousin was best man and dragged me along for support. But I was bored . . . so I slipped out to the gardens for a cigar . . .'

Lorel closed her eyes, turning her back on him, her heart thudding crazily against her breastbone. God, she could almost feel the wet grass beneath her feet again, see the distant lights of the hotel and hear the music flood out into the garden as she kissed Robert so passionately.

'It was the cigar smoke that gave me away, I suppose,' Steve Kennedy drawled thoughtfully. 'You saw me as Robert ran back to the hotel.'

It was flooding back to her now in waves, bringing nausea and disbelief. She swayed, her mind opening at last to bring back everything that had happened, everything she had wanted so badly to forget.

'You were furious,' Steve said lazily, watching her with those shrewd eyes. 'Hurling abuse at me. You certainly made my evening more interesting.'

'You should have told us you were there,' she said under her breath. 'You shouldn't have stayed to listen.'

'I was enjoying myself.' He stood in front of her now, hands in jeans pockets, his legs apart in a masculine pose of arrogance. 'I'd noticed you earlier, of course. At the ceremony. You were a pretty little thing. All that red hair . . . I was curious. And when you started kissing your brother-in-law . . .' he laughed, 'I was hooked!'

'How can you be so cruel?' Lorel's face was white as she stared at him. 'I was too young to know how to deal with my feelings. I was head over heels in love with him and he'd hurt me badly.'

His mouth twisted with sardonic malice. 'Of course,' he purred. 'And you'd play it all so differently now, wouldn't you?'

Her mouth trembled. 'I was eighteen!'

'A dangerous age!' he drawled, watching her from beneath hooded lids. 'And what a dangerous lady you turned out to be. Even I got a little burnt when I tried to play with you. Tell me—does your sister know?'

She blanched. 'Know what?'

'About the affair.' His eyes were brutal. 'I take it it's still going on?'

Lorel trembled, unable to trust herself to speak.

He nodded slowly, mouth tight. 'I thought so. Poor woman. I suppose she just turns a blind eye.'

'You don't know what you're talking about . . .' she whispered, hating him.

'You'd be surprised,' he drawled. 'Adultery has

the edge on other relationships, doesn't it? Or so I understand. I've always steered clear of it, personally. Too messy.'

She felt turned to ice, staring at him as though she was a statue, her body utterly still. He was standing in front of her, his body blocking her way to the door, or she would simply have run straight for it and out of this studio. It had been years. She hadn't ever thought about it. Locked it away at the back of her mind and changed her life so completely that there was no way back, no bridge to cross into her old life, and nothing to remind her of Steve Kennedy.

'I must admit you still look a million dollars.' Kennedy raked her from head to foot, a cynical smile on the hard mouth. 'I could still raise a fancy for you. I don't blame Robert for amusing himself with you.'

Her lids closed and she felt perspiration break out on her upper lip. 'Please go away,' she said almost inaudibly. 'I don't want to discuss this with you.'

'I'll bet you don't.' His mouth was hard. 'It's always alarming when an unwelcome part of your past rear its ugly head. But I'm afraid there's very little you can do. I'm here. Large as life and twice as ugly, and there's no way you're slipping away from me this time!'

Her eyes flashed open. 'I didn't slip away. I——'

'Four o'clock in the morning?' he said bitingly. 'Mean anything to you? A hotel room? A bed? A strange man lying next to you?'

'Oh, God . . .' she turned away, a hand to her mouth.

He watched her angrily, his jaw tight. 'I make you feel sick, do I? How nice! Shall I go on? Or do you need a moment to recover?'

She shook her head, whispering, 'I was drunk! I didn't know what I was doing!'

He gave a harsh crack of laughter. 'You could have fooled me!'

Lorel looked at him, bitter resentment in her eyes. 'I can remember wanting to slap your face then, and I wish now that I had!'

'At least you remember my face,' he said tightly. 'It's not very flattering to be forgotten by an ex-lover!'

That took her breath away. 'I was never your lover!'

'All right, then,' he said brutally. 'You were a one-night stand.'

She hit him then, as hard as she could, and her fingers stung under the impact. The slap echoed around the room. His head jerked back, black hair falling softly over his forehead.

Lorel stared at him in horror, her heart pounding a death march.

'I'm sorry . . .' she began, but it was too late and she leapt back with a cry as his hands shot out, tangling in her hair, tugging her towards him while she struggled, his face tight with rage.

His hard mouth came down over hers, forcing her lips apart as one hand clamped the back of her neck ruthlessly, his eyes fierce as the kiss deepened, making her heart beat as wildly as a captive bird's.

Bitterly, she flailed useless arms against his shoulders, tears burning her eyes as that hard body pressed her against the wall, his mouth inflicting a fierce combination of pain and pleasure on hers as she felt that tongue slide between her lips, his hands moving hard over her hips, his thighs pressing against hers.

'Remember me now?' he said tightly, against her mouth, then his lips were at her throat, hurting her, making her gasp as the white teeth bit her skin, making her lose all sense of reason as she tilted her head back, shivering as she felt that hot mouth slide over the base of her throat where a pulse throbbed. Then she started to struggle, desperate to break free and stop him.

He held her ruthlessly, then his mouth was back on hers, insistent, demanding, until she could scarcely breathe, and her legs almost gave way beneath her as her body flooded with heat in an overwhelming response and she despised herself.

Suddenly she was free, swaying, her eyes fevered as she stared uncomprehendingly at Steve, who was clearing his throat, pushing back thick black hair and calling sharply, 'Come in!'

Only then did Lorel realise someone had knocked on the door without her realising it.

'Oh . . .' A petite blonde with huge blue eyes stared at them. 'Not interrupting anything, am I?'

'Charlie!' Steve was immediately charm itself, sliding an arm around the over-feminine blonde. 'Not at all! I've been helping Miss Lane with her test.'

Charlie blinked false eyelashes and commented, 'She looks terrified. Are you sure you haven't been bullying the poor thing?'

'*Moi?*' Steve looked innocent, one hand splayed on his chest. 'Perhaps I was a little . . . forceful. But I coaxed a terrific performance out of her.'

Charlie observed Lorel closely, her tiny red mouth pursed. 'Looks bullied to me,' she said plainly.

Steve laughed. 'Just nervous, Charlie. A moment ago she was shaking from head to foot and quite breathless.' He slid an arrogant look at Lorel and raised his brows. 'So highly strung . . .'

Lorel's eyes flashed with silent hatred as she struggled for composure, her cheeks flushed and her mouth bruised. 'I might be too highly strung to cope with this whole thing,' she said tightly. 'I don't like the way you operate.'

'Can't stand the heat?' Steve drawled softly. 'Better get out of the kitchen. It's going to get a lot hotter.' He turned to Charlie, his tone once more businesslike. 'Send her to us in an hour, will you? And make her look like a nineteenth-century courtesan.'

Charlie nodded, studying Lorel's face. 'She has the mouth for it.'

Steve laughed derisively. 'Hasn't she just?' With that, he turned on his heel and left the room, closing the door behind him with a silent click. Lorel stared at the chipped white wood with hatred.

Charlie came over to her, turned her around and sat her in the make-up chair, scrubbing her face clean with an obsessive little look on her face, and pulling her red-gold hair back into a neat ponytail.

'I like Mr Kennedy,' Charlie said suddenly, bending her head to test colours on Lorel's hand, a wave of L'Air du Temps threatening to engulf Lorel as she did. 'He steamrollers people sometimes. But his heart's in the right place.'

Lorel gave her a look of sheer disbelief.

'Talented, too,' Charlie mused, head cocking to one side in a quick, sparrow-like movement. 'And sexy. Incredible when it all comes together like that.'

'Yes,' said Lorel stiffly. 'I suppose he is very talented.'

Talented at hurting other people, she thought angrily. It hadn't occurred to him that she might not want to remember him. Oh, no, of course it hadn't. Men like Steve Kennedy couldn't see past their own colossal egos. They didn't recognise the innermost feelings of other people, and felt quite cheerful about trampling over them at all times.

God, she remembered the last time he'd kissed her like that. And it had taken her breath away just as much. But she'd been drunk and unhappy and out of control. When she woke up in his hotel room at four in the morning wearing nothing but his dressing-gown, she had felt the deepest shame and self-hatred of her life.

Yes, she'd forgotten him. Deliberately wiped him out of her mind, and she supposed that could be seen as ruthless or unfeeling on her part.

But to wake up in a hotel room next to a naked stranger and be unable to remember how you got there or how many times you had made love to him was the most soul-destroying experience for any woman.

And as she'd looked at his dark head, the smudge of lipstick on his cheek, the tangled sheets that covered him to the waist, she had hated him only a little less than she had hated herself.

It was raining as she ran from the hotel, walking four miles in strappy evening shoes and a ridiculous taffeta ballgown. The country lanes were pitch-black and terrified her as she ran breathlessly, shivering with cold, her face wet with tears.

Shutting the front door, she had held her breath and listened in case her parents had woken up. All she could hear, though, was the soft tick of the grandfather clock and the hum of the central heating.

Otherwise, the house was silent and tranquil. It was five a.m. and she had behaved like a tramp, sleeping with a stranger in a seedy hotel room.

The safe, sunlit world of her childhood was suddenly threatened by the dark shadow of adult mistakes, and Lorel could not bear it.

She had tiptoed upstairs, slipping into her nightie and into her bed. She wanted no part of that other world, that disturbing adult world that pushed relentlessly into her mind, conjuring up images of a ruthless face, a hard mouth and long, sensual hands.

I don't want to remember! she had shouted in her head. I don't want to know! She had forced those disturbing images into the darkest corner of her mind she could find, and fallen into a heavy, dreamless sleep.

When she had woken in the morning, she'd remembered only the long walk home, coupled with brief, unsettling images of a tall, dark stranger. People had seen her dance with him, drink with him, and Lorel told herself that that was all it had been, just a harmless flirtation at her sister's wedding.

Within a month, she had successfully dismissed everything but the wedding ceremony and reception from her mind. Even her feelings for Robert had disappeared overnight. He was married and suddenly no longer capable of sweeping her off her feet. Married men, she'd discovered, were just too human to be exciting.

As for the dark stranger . . . he was nothing but a nightmare dreamt on a wild and stormy night, one she preferred not to think about.

Until Steve Kennedy burst back into her life like a whirlwind and *made* her remember.

Lorel swayed on to the set an hour later in heavy green silk, her shoulders bare. Technicians stopped dead as she passed, but she was oblivious to their stares, her eyes feverishly searching for Steve Kennedy among the crowd, unaware of the devastating combination of her wild red hair and full pink lips.

Steve looked up suddenly, turning that tanned, ruthless face towards her, and Lorel felt her heart jolt like an electric shock as his blue eyes narrowed on her.

Then she was on the stage, blinded by lights, surrounded by cables as the cameras began to roll and she found herself being turned this way and that, shot from every angle.

The test lasted four hours, during which she had to show every conceivable expression, and improvise various reactions crucial to the plot. When it was over, she felt drained, and retreated to her dressing-room, anxious to avoid Steve Kennedy at all costs.

Driving home, she thought obsessively about him. How dared he storm back into her life and turn it upside-down, shaking out all her darkest secrets?

Yes, she remembered him now. Oh, how could she have forgotten? She could almost hear the music of the wedding party as she slipped out through the open french windows and ran towards the cool sanctuary of the rose garden, tears burning her eyes . . .

Robert had followed her, and she had heard his footsteps behind her as she neared the shade of the trees.

'Lori!' His blond hair flopped as he ran, pale blue eyes watching her shadow dart between the long-fingered trees. 'Lori, wait!'

Breathless, she had turned, shivering in the strapless emerald evening gown, rain from the branches dripping on her bare shoulders as she watched Robert's tall, slender figure.

'Leave me alone, Robert!' she had said as he reached her, 'Can't you see what this is doing to me?'

'Lori, darling,' he said catching his breath as he reached her. 'Don't. I can't bear to see you so unhappy. Every man in that room would give his eye-teeth to be in my shoes right now—and you just ignore them all.'

She had laughed, eyes burning with tears. 'Don't try to flatter me, Robert. It's sweet of you, but it's hopeless. You know how I feel for you . . .' she broke off, biting her lower lip as she struggled for composure, turning her head away in sudden shame.

'I didn't mean to hurt you,' he said deeply.

Lorel shook her head, unable to speak.

'Forgive me.' He was drunk, his face flushed and perspiring as he watched her. Then, clumsily, he reached out and pulled her close to him, arms winding around her while she rested her head on his shoulder.

'I forgive you,' she said softly, smiling. At least they could still be friends.

'Poor little Lori,' Robert said in a slurred voice.

Lorel raised her head to look at him through wet lashes, then stood on tiptoe to place a chaste kiss on his mouth.

Robert watched her fixedly, then groaned and pulled her into his arms with sudden passion, his mouth descending on hers with a fierce demand that made her groan, her arms immediately winding around his head, hands pushing through his hair restlessly, all the pent-up emotion of the day rushing through her as she clung to him.

Then she realised what she was doing, and broke away from him, horrified. 'Robert, no!'

He stumbled backwards a little, staring at her, then flushed dark red, turned on his heel and ran back towards the house.

Tears burnt her eyes and she started to tremble, whispering, 'Oh, Robert! Oh, God, I love you so much!'

It was then that she smelt it. Saw the silver-blue wisp of smoke drift gently into the damp night air. Her body tensed with sudden horror and she whirled to face the shadows.

The glowing tip of the cigar moved slowly, and the dark hand that lifted it to a hard mouth gleamed with a white cuff, his face in total darkness save for the cold black glitter of his eyes.

'How long have you been there?' she breathed.

The shadow laughed softly, and his breath seemed to stir the leaves on the trees until they blended into one soft, mocking sigh.

'How long?' she demanded hoarsely.

'Long enough.' His voice was deep and strong, and he was as enigmatic as a highwayman in black mask and cape. 'I heard everything.'

Lorel whitened, unable to speak. Then she said fireraly, 'Why didn't you step forward? You should have told us you were there!'

He laughed, and at that moment the moon slid out from behind dark clouds, shining full on his face, showing the hard male bone-structure, the piercing blue eyes and the straight jut of his jaw.

'And spoil such a beautiful performance?' the stranger drawled mockingly. 'Absolutely not!' He flicked his gaze slowly over her bare shoulders, full breasts and slender waist. 'I liked the kiss the best,' he told her coolly. 'Very passionate. I'm looking forward to an action replay. Only with me on the receiving end.'

Lorel caught her breath, staring. 'Why, you . . .'

'I'd forgotten how passionate young girls could be,' he continued, eyes glittering with catlike malice. 'No wonder he followed you outside!'

Her cheeks flooded with hot colour. 'How dare you? I've got a good mind to have you thrown out of here!'

'Go ahead,' he drawled lazily. 'But if you do, I'll just have to tell someone exactly what I overheard.'

She whitened, unable to take her eyes off him.

'Your new brother-in-law!' he purred like a rattlesnake. 'I wonder what Daddy would say if he knew.'

Lorel swallowed, her mouth tight. 'You wouldn't dare,' she said in a low, trembling voice.

He laughed. 'I always accept a challenge,' he said softly. 'And I'm sure your father would be only too pleased to hear all about your love affair with Robert Stone.'

There was a long silence while she stared at him, green eyes bright with anger in her white face. Those heavy-lidded eyes looked sinister in this ethereal moonlight, and she didn't doubt for one moment that he would do it.

'Of course,' he said softly, 'you could always persuade me to keep my mouth shut.'

'That's blackmail!' she said furiously.

'Absolutely,' he drawled. 'But then I never could keep secrets.'

Lorel sucked in her breath, staring at him, her eyes bright green with rage. 'You contemptible swine . . .' She choked out, and her hand swung to slap his face, but he caught it in mid-air, his fingers biting into her wrist making her gasp and cry out.

'Well, well, well,' he drawled, ignoring her struggles and stepping closer, smiling lazily. 'So this is what happens when you're cornered. You come out spitting and fighting like a wildcat. Must be the red hair . . . I always thought that was an old wives' tale!'

Lorel struggled bitterly. 'I don't believe you know any old wives!'

'Kindly don't cast a slur on my mother's good name,' he said, smiling. 'She'd never forgive you.'

'Think you're funny, don't you?' Lorel was almost beside herself with rage. 'Well, I don't! And if you were my son, I'd disown you.'

'I don't doubt it,' he drawled softly. 'Which is why I'd rather be your brother-in-law. I can see just how rewarding that relationship could be!'

Lorel flinched, unable to fire back. They stared at each other for a long moment in tense silence. Then Lorel looked away, the wind whipping her red hair against her white face.

He loosened his grip. 'Have I hurt you?' he said

deeply.

'No!' she flared angrily, but tears stung her eyes
and her mouth trembled. Desperate to hide it, she
turned on her heel and ran back to the house, the
wind whipping her cheeks and bare shoulders, her
face flushed crimson as she re-entered the ballroom.

There was her father, drinking wine with a group
of friends, and Lorel stared at him with a slow
dawning of realisation. If the stranger told him
what he had heard, it would destroy Lorel. She
would never be able to live with it.

She bitterly regretted kissing Robert so
passionately—it had been a brief flare of madness,
and her guilt was colossal. If Pamela ever found
out, it would wound her deeply.

Desperate to take her mind off it, Lorel threw
herself into the celebrations, drinking far too much
as she danced from friend to friend, her red hair
flashing under the lights

As she whirled in emerald-green like a fiery
gypsy, she stumbled and almost fell, the clock
striking midnight with ominous chimes.

'Oh . . .!'

The strong arms that caught and held her were
the stranger's, and she stared at him in silence. In
this light, he was devastating. She noticed for the
first time that hard male face and its determined
jaw, the cool, straight mouth more sensual than
she had at first thought. His bone-structure was
razor-sharp, as were the piercing blue eyes.

'You're drunk,' he said coolly, standing perfectly

still in their private silence while Lorel's eyes drank him in.

Lorel looked at him defiantly, refusing to acknowledge the fierce thud of her heart. 'That's right!' she said with tense gaiety. 'Drunk, drunk, drunk,!' She twirled, eyes over-bright with laughter.

He caught her wrist and pulled her hard against him. 'Behave, little girl,' he drawled softly. 'People are staring.'

'Let them stare!' she flounced, and put out her tongue, feeling her pulses race as she carried on dancing. 'I've had a rotten day and an even more rotten night. Why shouldn't I enjoy myself.

He laughed. 'What are you drinking?'

'Champagne,' she said brightly. 'I love the bubbles. They're so . . . bubbly.'

'Perhaps you should switch to something less alcoholic,' he suggested. 'Like milk.'

Lorel stopped dancing and focused on him carefully. 'Has anyone ever told you how boring you are?'

'Not and lived to tell the tale,' he drawled.

'Well, you are,' she said haughtily. 'Exceedingly boring. No wonder you go around eavesdropping. I bet you're a peeping Tom, too. Where do you keep your binoculars?' She searched his dinner-jacket pockets, laughing. 'Not in there! Did you hide them in the plant pot?'

His eyes narrowed. 'That does it,' he said under his breath, and before she knew it he was forcing her off the dance-floor, his fingers an iron band around her wrist.

'Let me go!' she said with righteous indignation. 'I want to dance.'

'Dance?' he drawled, ignoring her furious struggles. 'You can hardly stand.'

People watched with amused smiles as they passed, and Lorel flushed to her roots, aware of what it must look like and hating the stranger for interfering.

'I'll call my father!' she threatened as he dragged her across the plush foyer.

'I believe we've already gone into that,' he told her lazily. 'And decided it was a bad idea.'

They had reached the brightly lit white steps of the hotel, and he took her outside into the darkness, the wind lifting his black hair as he spun her to face him.

'Sober up,' he said coolly. 'You're making a fool of yourself. Do you think Robert can't see what you're doing?'

She flushed angrily. 'How dare you?' she seethed, almost hopping with fury, 'I don't even know you—you're just a peeping Tom!'

'And you're a silly little girl who is playing with fire,' he said in a warning tone. 'Don't push me too far!'

'Why?' She danced about insolently. 'Will you fall over?'

His mouth tightened. 'You're asking for it,' he said under his breath, 'you know that?'

Lorel hiccuped. 'Do tell?' She swayed, her head suddenly rather fuzzy as the fresh air reacted badly

with the alcohol in her body. Her perception swung
violently, and she put out a hand to steady herself on
his broad shoulder, her flushed face going icy-cold.

'What is it?' he said deeply, his eyes intent on her
white face.

Lorel slowly raised her eyes to his. 'Oh, dear . . .'
she said carefully. 'I do feel rather strange . . .'

She woke up, her head spinning, to see the world
upside-down as steel lift doors closed behind her.
Very strange, she thought to herself, and drifted back
into oblivion, barely aware of the swaying motion as
she was carried along a silent corridor.

Next time she woke up, she was lying on a bed in a
strange bedroom, and the ceiling see-sawed violently,
so she closed her eyes, vaguely aware of a dark
shadow bending down over her.

'Robert . . .?' she whispered through dry lips, her
head throbbing as she put out a hand blindly to touch
thick hair, a strong pair of shoulders and a rough
jaw.

'Don't try to sit up,' said a deep, smoky voice, and
long hands slid to the side, pulling the zip of her
taffeta ballgown in one long, smooth motion.

Lorel obeyed, sinking back against the soft pillows
while his hands gently eased the dress down her body,
leaving her naked except for her peach silk cami-
knickers as the dress rustled softly to the floor.

'The room's going round and round,' she murmured, not daring to open her eyes.

He lifted her head gently. 'Just try not to think,' he
said softly, unclipping the gold necklace from her
throat and laying it on the bedside table. 'You'll be

fine in the morning.'

'Fine in the morning . . .' Lorel mumbled, and heard the light switch off, plunging the room into darkness.

'Goodnight,' the smoky voice said, and began to draw the quilt over her naked body.

Lorel put a hand over his and stopped him, whispering, 'Don't go.'

He froze, and she heard his heartbeat.

'I don't want to be alone,' she said innocently into the sudden electric silence. 'Stay with me, darling.'

There was a pause. 'Go to sleep,' he said roughly.

Lorel reached out her hand to run her fingers through his thick hair, caressing the back of his neck. 'Robert . . .' she said on a sigh. 'I do love you . . .'

He stiffened. 'You're drunk,' he said under his breath. 'I'm not Robert.'

She laughed softly. 'Silly Robert!' she whispered huskily, and traced the hard bones of his face with her fingers, running over his cheekbones and down to trail across his warm mouth. 'I'd know your face anywhere.'

He gave a sharp intake of breath. 'Don't . . .'

Lorel smiled. 'But I love you . . .' she whispered, and slowly lifted her head with her eyes shut to kiss his firm mouth, her full breast pressing against his chest.

'No . . .' he said thickly, his breath quickening, 'You don't know what you're doing.'

Lorel wound her arms around his neck. 'Oh, yes, I do.'

He groaned as she pulled him down to her, and lay totally still on top of her, his body rigid as his heart thudded against his ribcage.

'Just kiss me . . .' she murmured against his mouth, and he caught his breath as her lips met his, then he made a low, strangled sound from the back of his throat and those strong arms were around her, pressing her into the pillow as his mouth opened hers with hungry passion.

CHAPTER THREE

THE CALL came when she was in the bath at six o'clock. Lorel jumped, heart thudding, and scrambled out of the blue tub, splashing water all over the room as she dashed into the living-room stark naked.

She'd waited all her life for this call, and if she didn't get the part in the Luchino Piccardi picture, the disappointment would be awful. Even though she was prepared for failure, knowing Steve Kennedy would block her if he could, she still hoped with all her heart that this time she would be lucky, this time she would win.

'Hello?' Her voice was strained as she clutched the receiver, water dripping down her arm and on to the carpet.

'What took you so long?' drawled Steve Kennedy's dark voice.

'I . . .' Awareness of her nudity blazed over her, sending scarlet colour flooding to her face as she became overwhelmingly conscious of her full breasts and bare thighs. 'I . . . was in the bath.'

There was a silence. The line cracked. Then, 'I've seen the rushes. I'd like to meet with you to discuss them. Shall we say . . . one hour?'

Lorel thought fast, her heart thudding. 'Of course.

Does this mean I've got the part?'

'Be at my flat at seven,' he said lazily.

The line went dead and she glared at the phone for a long moment. Damn him! She slammed it down and stamped back into the bathroom. Why did he speak to her in that domineering way? Angrily, she got back into the tub and lay there brooding, listening to the shrieks and laughter of children playing outside in the courtyard below.

An hour later, she climbed the stairs to his flat, wind from an open window lifting her red-gold hair. The block was silent, save for the sound of cool, sexy jazz from inside Steve Kennedy's flat, the music muted by the closed door.

Lorel lifted one hand nervously, and knocked. Footsteps approached the door and she swallowed hard.

He swung the door back, studying her through hooded lids, his eyes glittering. 'Come in.'

He stepped back to allow her to pass, and she went in gingerly, careful not to brush her body against his. The hall was in semi-darkness, only the light from living-room illuminating them as they stood close to the front door while she closed it quietly behind her.

'Let me take your coat,' he said.

Lorel looked down at the blue silk dress she wore. 'But I'm not wearing a coat.'

'Well, let me take your dress, then,' he drawled and then his long fingers were sliding the top button of her dress undone to expose her lacey bra and the creamy swell of her breast.

'Stop that!' she burst out shakily, leaping back as

though scalded and doing the button up with trembling fingers. 'I came here to discuss my film test—not to play games with you.'

He laughed, studying her through hooded lids. 'It's your own fault,' he told her in that dark, smoky voice. 'You shouldn't have told me you were naked when I called this afternoon.'

'I didn't tell you anything of the sort!'

'You may take baths fully clothed,' he drawled, 'but I don't.'

'Well . . .!' Lorel floundered, cheeks flooding hot scarlet as she remembered the call, and felt naked again in front of him. 'I . . .'

He moved closer, making her back away, heart thudding. 'I thought about it all the way up the M1,' he murmured.

Lorel caught her breath, flustered, wishing she could slap his face, but afraid in case he pinned her to the wall and kissed the living daylights out of her again. He looked so damned attractive too, in the black jeans and white cashmere sweater, his black hair newly washed, curling damply at his neck.

'Look,' she said stiffly, 'I'm here on a professional basis. Please tell me whether I have the part or not, and I'll go.'

He studied her down that long, arrogant nose, his nostrils flaring. 'You start filming on Monday morning,' he said flatly. 'Or rather—you fly to Egypt on location on Monday.'

That took her breath away, and she stood staring as though in a dream, her lips slightly parted as she tried to believe it was actually happening, that she had actually done it, and was about to step into another life.

'Air Egypt will land us in Cairo. Filming begins on Tuesday.' He took a wallet from the back pocket of his jeans and handed it to her. 'In here you'll find your itinerary. Over the next five days you'll be rushed off your feet with costume tests, make-up tests and all the other paraphernalia for preparation. Think you can handle it? It'll be a tough schedule.'

Lorel nodded, feeling dazed. 'Yes, I think so . . .'

'You'd better know so before Monday morning,' he drawled. 'We can't afford to hire half-hearted actors.'

She lifted her chin, brows raised. 'I can handle it.'

He eyed her coolly. 'Ever been to Egypt? Africa?'

'No,' she shook her head, 'But I've always wanted to.' The romance and mystery of the Pharoahs had always attracted her, and she felt a thump of excitement at the prospect of seeing the Valley of the Kings, Karnack Temple, the Pyramids.

'I detect a dreamy look on your face,' he said coolly. 'Remove it. Egypt isn't all romance and drama. It's a very dangerous place, and a woman with your colouring will be abducted on sight if left unattended.'

Her mouth tightened with indignation. 'You make me sound like a suitcase. I'm not—I'm a human being.'

'A very attractive one, too,' he drawled softly stepping closer so that she backed away once more, heart thumping hard. 'All that red-blonde hair . . .' he murmured, lifting one long hand and running his fingers slowly through it. 'White skin . . . bright green eyes . . . you'd fetch at least thirty camels on the open market.'

'Very funny!' she snapped, trembling and a little breathless as she tried to escape. 'This is the late twentieth century—they're not barbarians!'

'They may not be,' he said with lazy amusement, 'but I am. And I could do with thirty camels!'

'Oh!' Scarlet with indignation, she pushed him away and opened the front door before he could stop her. 'I really must go now.'

'So soon?' he murmured, eyes mocking. 'And I was just beginning to enjoy myself!'

Lorel's mouth tightened. 'Thank you for giving me the news.' she said stiffly. 'I suppose I'll see you on Monday morning at the airport?'

'You bet your sweet life,' he drawled. 'I wouldn't miss this for the world. I can't wait to see how you cope with the heat, and dust and the insects.'

Her eyes flashed. 'I'm sure I'll manage!'

'I'll buy you a fly whisk,' he said coolly. 'And a bottle of mosquito repellent.'

'Looks like I'm going to be very popular,' she said angrily, 'what with the insects and the barbarians.'

His mouth twisted cruelly. 'And the ex-lovers!'

Lorel caught her breath, falling silent as she stared at him, her skin whitening as though from a physical blow. Slowly, she moistened her lips, and flushed as his narrowed eyes followed the quick movement.

'I told you,' she said huskily, 'I was drunk . . .'

'Or you wouldn't have let me lay a hand on you,' he said bitingly. 'I know all that. We went into that yesterday while you were busy remembering our night of passion!'

Lorel's face flooded with hot colour. 'It was a mistake! I can't even remember all of it now—just snatches . . .'

'Amuse me,' he drawled cruelly. 'Tell me which particular snatches you remember?'

Lorel bit back an angry retort, and told him the truth instead. 'I . . .' She turned her head away, unable to look at him. 'Only up until you kissed me . . .'

He gave a harsh crack of laughter. 'Kissed you where?' he drawled with catlike malice, and Lorel swallowed hard, her head bent with shame.

'On the bed . . .' she said huskily.

'Good,' he purred. 'It's all coming back to you. What exactly were you wearing at the time?'

Lorel closed her eyes. 'Nothing,' she whispered.

He bent his head and drawled, 'Sorry? Could you say that again?'

She lifted her head. 'Nothing!' she flung bitterly, tears stinging her eyes, and she whirled, opening the front door and almost falling out, her legs weak beneath her, her face hot with shame as she stumbled out into the corridor.

He watched her go, his face grim, and did not try to stop her as she ran into the hall and down the stairs, almost falling over her feet fleeing into her own flat as though the hounds of hell were after her.

'Be on that plane,' Steve bit out as she ran, 'or you're out of the picture. Got it?'

Lorel didn't answer or look up at him, simply ran

into her own flat and slammed the door behind her, leaning against it, heart pounding and legs almost giving way.

Was that how it would be? In Egypt? For the whole of the film? This film could take a year to make or more. Would Steve hound her for the whole year?

The contract was signed the following day in Luchino Piccardi's Sloane Square office.

From the moment her pen touched the paper, she was whisked off her feet, whirlwinded into action with costume tests, make-up tests, God knew how many different tests. Then there were injections and travelling insurance and money, plus calls to her family and friends to let them know where she was going and with whom. Her feet didn't touch the ground. She worked almost eighteen hours a day trying to get everything organised.

Steve Kennedy was rarely seen—she once caught a glimpse of him at Elstree Studios, running out of a sound stage and across the car park, his long legs and muscular body perfectly co-ordinated, black hair lifting in the wind as he ran, eyes narrowed against the cold.

Lorel had stood and watched from the costume-fitting window, saw him bend to a low-slung black Jaguar XJS sports car, get in and shoot out of the car park with a squeal of tyres. She was half disappointed that she hadn't seen him, and couldn't understand why.

. By Sunday she was exhausted. She spent the morning at the studio going over the script with her coach, but was given the afternoon off. They wanted their cast fresh when they arrived in Cairo.

Lorel got home to find Mary waiting for her with a bottle of champagne and a box of chocolates.

Lorel sank back on the sofa, exhausted, and closed her eyes while Mary opened the champagne, pouring two frothy glasses out and offering her chocolates.

'A double celebration,' said Mary, sitting on the sofa opposite. 'I've just landed a part in *Peter Pan* at Bournemouth Christmas panto.'

'Oh, well done!' Lorel was delighted to know that her friend would not feel left behind when Lorel took off for Cairo, fame and fortune.

'It's a small part,' said Mary, munching a coffee cream. 'Well—minuscule, really! But I've also got an audition with the BBC for an Alan Jeffries play they're doing next year. My agent says the part's perfect for me.'

They settled down a moment later to watch the video Mary had got specially, one of Lorel's favorites—*Wuthering Heights*.

'Heathcliff!' cried Merle Oberon, struggling across rain-drenched moors while thunder and lightning crashed all around her. 'Heathcliff!'

Mary sniffed and ate another coffee cream.

The telephone rang and Lorel fumbled for it in the dark, one eye on the television screen.

'Hello?' she said vaguely.

'Lori?' Robert's voice was husky as it came over the line. 'It's me.'

'Oh, hello, Robert.' she said, smiling. 'What can I do for you? It's ages since I heard from you.'

'Lori . . . it's Pam. There's been an accident.'

Lorel froze, her whole body stiffening as she waited in appalled silence, unable to speak or breath as she heard the line crackle, the noise from the television continue stupidly in the background.

'She fell downstairs,' Robert told her thickly, 'about an hour ago. I only left her for a second . . . she'd been complaining all afternoon about a stomach ache—I thought it was indigestion. How was I to know? We had such a heavy lunch . . .'

Lorel waited, her face drained of all colour, still unable to speak in case she heard something she desperately did not want to hear. She saw Pam in her mind's eyes, so pretty and full of life, with all that red hair, vivacious smile and big blue eyes.

'I ran downstairs to get her some aspirin—I had no idea how much pain she was in. I was such a fool . . .' He drew a ragged breath, forcing himself to go on. 'I was just going into the kitchen when I heard her cry out, then there was a second's silence and . . . she fell. Just crashed all the way down . . . it was so sickening, Lori.'

'She's not . . .' The question flew from her lips.

'No!' Robert shuddered, his voice husky as he continued, 'But my God, it was a close call. If only she'd told me how much pain she was in! It was appendicitis, you understand. Acute appendicitis. They only just got her on the operating table in time.' He laughed and added, 'Maybe it was a blessing she fell when she did. At least it got her into hospital.'

Lorel ran a hand over her eyes and said huskily, 'She hates hospitals.'

'It could have been so easy . . . a quick operation,

a few stitches . . . now look what she's done. And all because she hates hospitals.'

'What did the hospital say?' Lorel asked.

Mary got up, her face pale, and switched the sound down on the television, leaving Heathcliff and Cathy silently battling it out on the black and white moors.

'That she was lucky,' Robert said deeply. 'The appendicitis alone could have killed her.'

'But is she going to be all right?'

He sighed heavily and his voice broke. 'Depends what you mean by all right. Her leg was broken—I could tell that at a glance. It was kind of at right angles to her body, like a puppet's . . .' He gave a raw gasp and said tightly, 'Lorel, I don't think I can manage here on my own. You've got to come down. Please.'

She stared at the telephone cord twisted around her finger and said, 'I can't. I'm flying to Egypt tomorrow.'

'Egypt!' There was a long silence and the line crackled. 'What on earth for?'

'A film.' Her eyes stared unseeingly at the wall. 'Didn't Pam tell you?'

'Yes . . .' he said vaguely. 'Yes, she did mention something about a film . . . but Lori, I just can't manage here. The twins are—well, they're not stupid. They saw it happen. It was so fast and everything just turned into chaos. I tried to keep them away, but they saw everything. Pam falling, the ambulance taking her away . . .' He laughed shakily. 'Me cracking up.'

Lorel bit her lip, torn by the vivid scene that

flashed into her mind of the twins. 'Poor little mites. How are they taking it?'

'I'm not sure. They're only three, and I can't remember being three, so I can't see inside their heads. But they're jittery and fractious. Billy wouldn't eat his tea and Babs is pink and getting noisier by the minute.'

Lorel closed her eyes. How could she leave for Egypt knowing Robert and the twins were in trouble? Knowing Pam was lying in hosiptal, barely able to move? She desperately wanted to help.

'Lori, please,' Robert said desperately. 'Please come down here. I need your help. With your parents away in Philadelphia and mine long since gone . . . there's just no one else I can turn to.'

She almost wept. Torn apart, she stared wildly into space, unable to make a decision. She couldn't let this happen to Robert, Pam and the twins. She just couldn't. Even though there might never be another chance to make a film this good, she knew in her heart that she could not turn her back on her family. Not when they needed her this badly.

'I need you,' Robert urged. 'We all do. Please—please help.'

'I . . .' Her voice broke, but she steeled herself to be strong, her jaw tightening as she said tautly, 'I'll be there some time this evening. It shouldn't take longer than three hours.'

Robert almost wept with relief, and a moment later, when Lorel put the telephone down, so did she. The tears burnt the back of her eyes and she stood up.

'Oh, Lorel . . .' Mary said softly when she told her. 'I'm so sorry. If there's anything I can do . . .?'

Lorel shook her head, mouth trembling. 'Nothing. I wish there was.'

Resolutely, she went into her room and refused to cry, feeling as though she'd just lost everything. She flung clothes into a tiny suitcase, her heart aching as she saw the array of suitcases already packed for Egypt with such excitement and optimism, filled with bright, summery clothes, straw hats and strong, flat sandals.

She sighed, rolled up her sleeves and got on with it. An hour later she was ready to leave, and went back into the living-room to find Mary busy in the kitchen making a flask of hot coffee and packing a sandwich for her to eat on the motorway.

'Thanks.' Lorel took them and put them in her hold-all.

'Here,' Mary said, 'take the tartan rug . . . it'll keep you warm.'

Lorel dimpled, saying affectionately, 'Don't fuss, Mother Hen.'

Mary made a face. 'Will if I want to.' She studied Lorel, the smile fading from her lips as she said quietly, 'What are you going to do about Mr Kennedy?'

Lorel's heart leapt at the sound of his name. He would be trouble. With a capital T. 'I'll leave him a note,' she said huskily. 'I can't face him.'

She hastily scrawled an explanatory note and sealed it in an envelope before she could change her mind. Running up to his flat, she pushed it through the letter-box together with the tickets for Egypt and the itinerary and work schedule. She wouldn't be needing them now.

Turning from his door with a sinking heart, she went back to her own flat, got her suitcase and left. Mary walked her to the car, wrapped in her white fur-collared coat.

It was raining quite heavily, and the orange glow of the street lights was reflected in the puddles on black tarmac. Cars shot past on the main road opposite. A bus chugged by, big and red and lit up, with people staring gloomily out of steamed-up windows.

'Drive carefully, won't you?' Mary said quietly. 'The motorways are so dangerous in this weather.'

Lorel nodded. 'Don't worry, I'll . . .'

She broke off as a low-slung black Jaguar XJS sports car drew up a few yards behind her.

Steve Kennedy stepped out, tall and dark and sexy in a black cashmere coat and white silk evening scarf, his face tanned and razor-sharp as he walked beneath the street light, going round to the other side of the car.

The woman who stepped out, sliding her hand in his, wore a full-length black mink coat and had gold-blonde hair and perfect blue eyes, her mouth a cool, red pussycat smile as she looked up at him and murmured something huskily.

Steve laughed and bent his head to kiss her full on the mouth.

Lorel felt slightly sick and kept totally still in case they saw her. She watched them walk into his flat building and close the door.

'Well . . .' Lorel said, starting the engine, 'I don't think he's going to be too bothered when he finds that note!'

Mary smiled. 'What a stroke of luck! At least now you won't feel too guilty!'

Lorel gave her a frozen smile. 'A stroke of luck,' she agreed tightly, and reversed, waving. 'See you soon!'

'Ring when you get there so I know you're safe!' Mary called, her voice high and clear in the empty London street.

Lorel drove straight on to the motorway. So that was the kind of man Steve Kennedy was! How dared he accuse her of callousness when he had kissed her so passionately, made so many open advances to her—and all the time had a ravishing woman like that on his string. He really did take the biscuit!

The endless motorway lights flashed past, blurred by rain and the irritating click-clack of windscreen wipers. She listened to various tapes as she drove down, passing through each county with relief, until she finally saw the small blue sign with the coat of arms flash past under her headlights saying 'Wiltshire'. She almost cheered out loud.

Then she was driving through country lanes, past tiny villages until she found Laysham, and eventually turned along the small farm road that lead to her sister's house.

The lights were on, and the small Tudor house was welcoming in spite of its recent traumas. Lorel parked the car, stretched her aching arms and back, and plunged out the headlights.

As she stepped out of the car, her legs stiff, the front door opened and light spilled out on to the charming little garden path littered with shrubs and flowers and plants.

Slamming the boot, she looked up through the driving rain to see Robert standing in the doorway, his face etched with strain.

'Lorel . . .' He stepped out, walking down the wet path to take her suitcase from her. 'Thank God! I thought you'd never get here.'

'How is she?' Lorel walked with him to the warm, welcoming house. 'Have you heard?'

'The operation was a success.' He shouldered into the house and put her case down, running a hand through wet blond hair. 'But the list of injuries from the fall . . .'

Lorel listened in silent disbelief as he ran through a litany containing a broken left leg, severed bruising to face and ribs, two fractured fingers and a fractured ankle. Her face paled and she closed her eyes. 'Poor Pam.'

When she looked up again it was to see two tiny blond imps sitting huddled on the stairs in their Christopher Robin matching dressing-gowns, one red, one blue.

Lorel grinned at them and they grinned back. Robert caught the look and turned his head.

'What are you two doing up?' he demanded in mock thunder. 'Get back to bed at once!'

'We want to see Auntie Lolly!' piped up Babs, big blue eyes daring her father to send her to bed. 'We haven't seen her for a milion years.'

Lorel laughed. 'I sound like a dinosaur!'

The twins scampered down the stairs and bounded all over Lorel, their faces flushed and pink.

'Come on, now,' Robert said sternly. 'Back to bed!'

Reluctantly, they climbed back up the stairs. Lorel watched them go, smiling, then turned to Robert and slipped her coat off, hanging it on the dark, polished-wood coatstand.

'I'm exhausted. Any chance of a cup of tea?'

Robert clapped a hand over his mouth. 'God, how stupid of me! I am sorry. Wait here, I'll put the kettle on.'

Lorel smiled, watching him dart into the kitchen. Behind her she heard the calm tick-tock of the grandfather clock her parents had given Pamela a year ago. The smile faded from her lips as she studied it, the dark wood grandfather clock with its round gold face and long shiny pendulum. It had been there in her parents' house the night Pam got married . . . the night Lorel met Steve.

A shiver ran over her. She had thought she had buried him—but he had come back. Her eyes darkened. This time, though, there would be no reappearances. He wouldn't come back for her after this. She didn't know why, but that knowledge made her heart heavy, and her eyes sad.

Robert came back at a rush, heading for the living-room, but stopped when he saw her, and his brows drew in a quick frown.

'Anything wrong?' he asked slowly, watching her cool remote face.

'Oh!' Startled, she turned, and her green eyes reflected her confusion as she pushed away the images in her head, the blue eyes and forceful jaw, the hard mouth and long, punitive fingers. 'I'm fine. Fine.'

Robert was silent for a moment, then stepped towards her. 'Do you mind very much?' he asked softly. 'About the film?'

Lorel stared into his handsome face, thought of Steve Kennedy going into his apartment with the blonde-haired beauty, picking up her note while the woman slung her black mink over a chair, scanning it with those narrowed eyes then crumpling it up and throwing it away. Perhaps his jaw would tighten, or his eyes flare with temper for a moment. But tomorrow he would be on the plane to Egypt, a replacement actress would be called in, and Lorelei Lane would be erased from their lives.

'Yes,' she said huskily, 'I mind very much.'

Robert was silent, at a loss for words.

'But I'd mind a lot more,' Lorel said slowly, 'if I were in Egypt worrying about Pam. About you and the twins.' She gave him a wry smile. 'There'll be another film, Robert. But you're the only family I've got.'

CHAPTER FOUR

LOREL woke up disorientated, staring at the sloping beamed ceiling for a moment with complete acceptance. Then she frowned, turned her head, and saw the rolling Wiltshire countryside outside her window, the fierce, clear light shining on the rainwashed land, making the colours sharp and extraordinarily rich, as though each tree, each hedge, each patch of dark, damp earth had been newly painted and left out to dry in the sun. Birds sang outside, and no traffic disturbed the peace of this village. It was silent and untouched by the twentieth century.

Lorel focused on the clock and felt a stab of sadness. Eight-thirty . . . they would be at the airport, checking in, going excitedly to await their call in the lounge, drinking coffee, and discussing avidly the sights awaiting them in Egypt.

She allowed herself that precious moment of regret. The she pushed back the duvet and got up, slipping a pink silk négligé over her matching nightie and stepping into her slippers.

Downstairs, bedlam reigned. Robert was desperately trying to shave and eat his toast at the same time, the electric razor buzzing noisily but drowned out by the twins, who banged their spoons on the table, chorusing in unison, 'We want brekfussed!'

Robert turned as Lorel came in. 'These little pests are making my life a misery—can you fix their breakfast before I fix them?'

'Nasty Daddy!' said Babs, putting her tongue out.

Lorel smiled and went over to the water boiling on the stove. 'Boiled eggs, I take it?'

Robert nodded. 'It seemed easiest.'

Lorel put two eggs in the water and popped a couple of slices of break in the toaster. A newspaper thudded on to the mat and she heard the paper boy whistling as he walked back down the path.

'You're off to work, then?' Lorel observed as she watched Robert gulp down tea and a mouthful of toast and marmalade. 'You could easily take the day off, you know. I'm sure other people would.'

He made a face. 'I'd only mope all day. Work will keep my mind off it, and I can't visit her until three this afternoon. Honestly! What a little Hitler that Sister is! You should have heard the way she spoke to me—I felt like a leper.'

Lorel followed him to the front door as he rushed up the hall, picking up his briefcase on the way, looking harassed and preoccupied.

'Drive carefully,' she said as Robert pulled open the front door. 'One accident in the family is quite enough.'

He stopped, relaxing enough to give her a smile. 'Am I all strung-up?' he asked quietly.

She nodded, eyes dancing. 'I can see the ropes from here.'

He studied her in silence, the light from the sun shining down over his blond hair, and the cool winter wind blowing through the open door, making Lorel shiver, draw her négligée closer to her.

'Thanks for coming, Lori,' he said huskily. 'You've really saved our lives.'

'Off you go,' Lorel said firmly, parting his arm. 'I'll ring you if there's any news.'

Robert smiled, and bent his blond head to kiss her cheek, then raced out to his car. Lorel closed the door and went back into the kitchen with the newspaper to find the twins involved in an argument.

'Stop it!' she said sharply as Babs tried to poke Billy's eyes out with her spoon. 'Breakfast is coming.' Spooning the boiled eggs into two fat friar smiling egg cups, she cut the buttered toast into thin strips and put the plates on the table. 'Egg soldiers!' she said proudly.

Billy eyed his egg dolefully. 'Me can't like eggs,' he said in a quiet little voice.

'I'll have his!' Babs offered, making a grab for it.

Lorel smacked her hand lightly. 'What would you like instead, Billy?'

'Um . . .' Billy looked thoughtful. 'Cornflakes would be nice.'

Lorel got his cornflakes and handed them to him a moment later, watching him munch them as he stared off into space in his own little world.

The doorbell rang and Lorel sighed, going down the hall to answer it, seeing the tall, dark shadow framed by sunlight through the glass-topped door, and registering just a fraction of a second too late that that shadow was far too tall to be Robert.

'Oh!' She swayed, breathless, staring into Steve

Kennedy's narrowed blue eyes as she pulled the door open.

He towered over her, looking rich and sexy in a black cashmere jumper and black trousers, a red tartan scarf at his throat, and a black cashmere overcoat, with the collar pulled high against the cold.

They stared at each other in silence as the wind whipped strands of black hair from his tanned forehead.

'How did you find me?' she asked breathlessly.

Shivering, she was unconscious of the sensuality of her appearance, barefoot in the thin silk nightdress, her face softened by sleep and no make-up, her long red-gold hair tumbling in tousled curls at her shoulders.

'With great difficulty,' he told her in a deep voice. 'May I come in?'

Lorel studied him nervously. A ferocious lion on her doorstep and he wanted to come in. 'Of course . . .' she said huskily, stepping back and watching him enter. 'Can I take your coat?' she offered, then flushed hotly as his eyes met hers with derisive mockery, reminding her of the time he'd said that to her.

Slowly, he unbuttoned it with long, tanned fingers and slid it from his powerful shoulders, muscles flexing beneath the black cashmere jumper.

'So . . .' he said softly, watching her through hooded lids, 'you've thrown away your career. And I'm here for an explanation.'

She moistened her lips, pulses skipping. 'Yes, of course,' she said huskily, 'I would have explained in my note, but I didn't know how to say it all on paper.'

'And now we're face to face,' he murmured. 'So it should be easy.'

She nodded, running a trembling hand through her red-gold hair. He was so calm, so still. It unnerved and alarmed her. 'Robert called me yesterday afternoon,' she said. 'He was distraught. My sister had fallen downstairs and been rushed to hospital with appendicitis and serious injuries.'

Steve pursed his lips, frowning. 'I'm sorry. Is she recovering?'

Lorel shrugged. 'As well as can be expected.'

'Go on,' he said softly.

'What more is there to say?' she asked huskily. 'I had to drop out of the film and come at once.'

He nodded, studying her icily. 'And your decision had nothing to do with your previous feelings for Robert Stone?'

Lorel shook her head, frowning. 'Oh, no. It may look like that, I admit——'

'But you're no longer in love with him,' he drawled softly through his teeth, 'and wouldn't even consider adultery!'

She caught her breath, staring. 'No!'

'Of course not,' he drawled with catlike malice. 'That's why you kissed him so adoringly on the doorstep!'

'I . . .' She blanched, staring with horrified eyes. 'My God, you were watching!'

'That's right,' he said under his breath, and his eyes flashed a warning of rage. 'What a charming little domestic scene! The beautiful wife kissing husband goodbye on the doorstep! Straight out of

Hollywood.'

Her face flamed with hot colour. 'That's not——'

'No, it's not, is it?' he said tightly, advancing on her, 'Because in this case it happens to be the beautiful mistress kissing her adulterous lover goodbye——'

'Shut up!' Lorel burst out hotly, shaking. 'You have no right——'

'I have every right!' he said, his jaw tight with anger. 'You ran out on my film, cost me thousands of dollars and made me look a bloody fool for hiring you in the first place!'

'I had to put my family first!' she flared, heart in her mouth.

'Like hell you did!' he bit out, 'You jumped at the chance to move in with him! Has he succumbed to temptation yet? It looked like it from where I stood!' He laughed angrily, eyes flashing over her body.

Hot colour flooded over her face and she glared at him, pulling her négligé tightly to her throat to hide the full breasts that strained at the silk and lace of her nightdress.

'Get out of here!' she breathed, hurt more than she could bear by his cruel words. 'And take your disgusting accusations with you!'

'Accusations,' he said fiercely, 'not actions. After what you've done to your own family, I coud kill you and not feel a thing!'

'Do you think I care,' she flung bitterly, 'what you think of me?'

His mouth trembled with rage. 'Don't care,' he said tightly, 'was made to care!'

And then he was coming for her, murder in his eyes while she cried out, backing away from him until her feet hit the stairs and she stumbled, scrambling to her feet, eyes wide as she ran for her life so stupidly up the stairs.

He caught her at the top, and they fought in bitter silence, only their breathing speaking volumes between them. Her heart hammered violently as she pushed at his shoulders, fists raining impotent blows, trying to hit his dark face, but it was implacable, and the fury in the hard line of his mouth made her shrink away from him, eyes wide with fear.

'Don't!' she cried breathlessly as he swept her off her feet and carried her, kicking and slapping, into a bedroom, kicking the door open with one swift blow and throwing her on the bed.

'Do you think I enjoy being made a fool of?' he said under his breath as he pinned her to the bed, the bright scarlet tartan scarf unknotted in their struggle, showing the tanned column of his throat and the network of black hairs on his dark chest.

'For God's sake!' she gasped, trying to reach him beyond his anger. 'It isn't what you think . . . there's no affair . . . I'm not in love with him!'

'Do you think I was born yesterday?' he snapped.

'Very probably,' she said, tears stinging the back of her eyes and her mouth trembling as his fingers bit into her arms, holding her prisoner, 'or you wouldn't think me capable of it!'

His eyes flickered and he said tightly, 'I've seen the evidence with my own eyes!'

'You only think you have,' she said huskily, tears

welling in her eyes. 'Do you honestly think I could do that to my own sister? With my niece and nephew under the same roof? What sort of woman do you think I am?'

There was a long, tense silence, and he studied her with narrowed eyes, his jaw tight as he breathed harshly. Lorel lay looking up into his angry face, her red-gold hair fanning out against the brightly coloured patchwork quilt. She hoped desperately that he wouldn't kiss her, because she knew only too well what had happened the last time he had—she'd lost control and responded feverishly. Not only did she resent that strange power he had over her, but she didn't understand and didn't want to. Lying on this bed, beneath his strong arms, she felt in a very dangerous position indeed.

'Then why did you kiss him?' he asked finally. 'Why are you wandering about in satin and lace? Why does something so supposedly innocent look so damning?'

She closed her eyes and said breathlessly, 'He's desperately worried about Pam . . . you must see how he feels . . . everything in his life revolves around her . . . he was falling apart last night when I got here.' She stopped, looking at him through her lashes. 'He blames himself. He knew she didn't feel well, yet he didn't call a doctor.'

His eyes narrowed. 'That doesn't answer my question! Why did he kiss you?'

She sighed. 'He was grateful to me,' she said. 'That's all.'

He watched her in brooding silence, his face

shuttered and unreadable.

Lorel's fingers curled helplessly on his broad shoulders. 'Well,' she said huskily, 'do you believe me?'

His mouth hardened and he sat up, looking away. 'I don't know what to believe,' he said flatly, and ran a hand through his thick, black hair: 'You're very convincing.'

Lorel sat up slowly, studying the back of his black head as he stared with unseeing blue eyes through the criss-cross lattice windows that backed on to the Wiltshire downs.

'I'm telling the truth,' she said quietly.

'You're also a damned good actress.' He looked at her, the blue eyes still angry. 'Why else do you think I'm here? We need you in that film, Lorel. There's no one else—not at this short notice.'

She looked down, lashes sweeping the vulnerable curve of her cheek. 'I'm sorry . . .' she began huskily.

'Sorry?' His voice shook. 'Can I quote you on that!'

She gave him an angry look. 'I don't believe you're that stuck without me! I know at least twenty actresses who'd give their eye-teeth for that role!'

'I know at least twenty thousand,' he drawled. 'But they don't have your screen presence or your talent.'

She eyed him in silence for a moment. 'You're just trying to flatter me.'

'No.' He shook his dark head, his face very serious. 'You almost burnt the celluloid in that screen test, Lorel. I don't know what it is, but you've got it.'

Lorel was stunned, unable to reply.

'We want you to fly out to Egypt,' Steve went on deeply, 'when all this is sorted out. Luchino is prepared to hold your scenes for you. We can shoot around you until you get there.'

She caught her breath, staring at the dark profile in astonishment. So all her work had not been in vain, all that training and hoping and wishing. Also, she had misjudged Steve Kennedy. Not only had he not stood in her way over this part, but he was prepared to drive two hundred miles to get her to agree to going ahead with the role.

'I . . .' she floundered. 'It might be weeks before Pam gets out of hospital.'

'We can wait.' he said firmly.

'Well . . .' she said huskily, 'my answer is yes, then. I wouldn't miss the chance of working in that film for all the world.

He stood up slowly, walked to the small white table and picked up the silver-framed photograph.

It was Robert and Pamela on their wedding day, standing in front of the church, laughing as confetti drifted over their heads.

'Beautiful couple,' he murmured, studying it. 'A pity they didn't realise what would happen in the end.'

Her mouth tightened and she glared at him. 'I thought we'd settled that?'

His gaze flicked to hers coolly. 'You were wrong.' He replaced the photograph with a cool click and walked back to her. 'I have to go. Will you see me to the door?'

Lorel stood up with an imperceptible sigh and followed him to the bedroom door and down the stairs, watching the back of his black head and wondering why he was so obstinate in his belief that she was having an affair with Robert. But what would she herself believe, if she was in his shoes? She had to admit the evidence so far must look pretty damning. But she had genuinely come down here to look after Robert and the children until Pam was better. How could she prove that to Steve—more important, why should she want to?

'Is there a hotel nearby?' Steve asked, shouldering into his black cashmere coat, buttoning it with slender fingers, pulling the collar up at his throat and fastening the scarlet tartan scarf tightly, a blaze of colour against the sombre black.

'In the village,' Lorel replied automatically. 'The White Swan.' Her eyes widened as she realised what he was about to do and she took the last three stairs at a breathless rush. 'You're not staying here, are you?'

'Of course!' He pulled black leather gloves on his hands and flexed them. 'You don't seriously expect me to disappear and leave you alone with your darling brother-in-law?'

Lorel stared in disbelief. 'But . . .'

'Every time I see you and Robert Stone together, you're in each other's arms.' He studied her obliquely through thick black lashes. 'The fact that I disapprove strongly of what you're doing is neither here nor there.'

'Well, you said it!' she retorted furiously.

'But Cavalcade Films will also not see it in a good light. If you're ever going to make something of yourself, you're going to have to control your behaviour to some degree. We don't want a scandal erupting around you. Particularly not one involving your sister's husband.'

Her mouth tightened, and she studied him in angry silence for a moment before saying tightly, 'You're never going to believe me—are you?'

He gave her a cool, sardonic smile. 'I doubt it.'

Their eyes met and warred.

'Well,' Lorel said flatly, hating him, 'there's not much point in my trying to deny it any longer, is there?'

There was a long, tense silence, and she saw the mocking laughter fade from his eyes, darkening them until they were almost black as he stared at her through hooded lids. His mouth thinned, and she saw a muscle start to jerk in his tanned jaw.

'You admit it, then?' he said tightly.

Lorel studied him icily. 'I admit nothing. I merely said——'

'Answer me, yes or no!' he flared, rage sparking in his eyes to such a degree that she jumped and took a step back, studying him, wide-eyed. 'Are you having an affair with him?'

Heart thumping, Lorel said shakily, 'No . . . I told you before . . .' Her throat closed convulsively, and she shook her red-gold head. 'There's nothing between Robert and me.'

He watched her in silence, the blue eyes narrowed. Then he nodded. 'Good.' And he turned on his heel, pulled open the front door and walked out, striding down the front path without a backward glance, his black hair lifting in the icy wind, black cashmere coat flapping apart as he went to the car, the scarlet scarf a blaze of colour as it flew behind his black figure.

Lorel clung to the door-handle, watching him. 'You can't book into that hotel!' she called after him pleadingly. 'I don't want you to stay!'

He had reached the car parked just beyond the thick hedges, and he looked at her over the roof of it with narrowed blue eyes.

'Too bad!' He opened the door, slid in the front seat, started the car with a roar of discreet power and a moment later shot away down the narrow country road, even the trees on either side seeming to bow to him as he passed.

Damn him! Lorel slammed the front door and leaned on it with her eyes closed. Why does he affect me like this? Why is he the only person I've ever met who can get inside my bloodstream and make me react like that?

Lorel shook her head as though to rid herself of his face and presence. Then she went into the kitchen, finding the twins watching breakfast TV. Taking them upstairs, she bathed and dressed them ready for their playgroup in the village.

Steve Kennedy was an obstinate as he was selfish, and there was nothing she could do to stop him if he intended to stay here and cause trouble.

She gritted her teeth, brushing Billy's hair while he cringed away from the comb, hating every minute of it. How could he think her capable of having an affair with Robert? Under the very same roof as the twins. It would be despicable, and she hated him for believing her capable of it. But then—he didn't really know her, did he?'

She stopped, in the middle of pulling Billy's jumper over his head, leaving him stuck inside it, headless and armless.

What did she know about him, either? That he was a talented and ambitious screenwriter, wealthy and successful, who wielded power with a practised hand. He was arrogant, but he was also witty. He did at least have a sense of humour, she had to give him that. He was selfish and overbearing—but he was also generous, and gave praise freely when he thought it was due.

Lorel sighed, frowning. He was a complex man, and the only thing that really bothered her about him was his power of attraction. The fact that he could, with one kiss, make her head swim and her legs turn to jelly, made her feel on edge every time he was around.

'Me stuck in here,' said a little voice, and Lorel blinked, snapping out of her thoughts.

She bit her lip. 'Poor Billy!' and pulled the jumper down over his head for him.

Driving the twins to the playgroup, she passed the White Swan and saw Steve's car outside it, which made her heart thud too fast as she put on a little speed.

What had happened between them was one of the main reasons she hated him. It was hard to forgive herself for making love to a stranger. And knowing he was here, in town, where it all happened five years ago, made it harder.

'I'm home!' Robert slammed the front door at six o'clock, and Lorel looked up from the oven where the vegetables were simmering in their various pans.

'How is she?' she called, opening the kitchen door.

His face was strained as he walked in. 'Dazed and shaken. I don't think she's taken it all in yet. Her leg's in plaster and her face is covered in bruises. She just sort of mumbled a lot while I was there.' He sighed, running a hand through his blond hair. 'If only there was something I could do to cheer her up.'

Lorel studied his anguished profile and put a hand on his arm comfortingly. 'Don't worry, Bobby. She'll get better. Did the hospital have any news about her? When she'll be out?'

He looked irritated. 'They were no help at all. Said she'd be back to her normal self in a week or so, but they couldn't possibly commit themselves to a date for release.'

Lorel bent to open the oven and inspect the lamb, which smelt delicious. 'When can I visit her?'

'Whenever you like. Tonight?'

'Lovely. I'll get changed after dinner.'

She served dinner and called the twins, who were playing on the floor in the hall with Billy's train set. Babs had tied one of her dolls to the tracks and they were waiting gleefully for a major rail disaster to happen as the electric train sped towards the doll.

She arrived at the hospital just after seven, and eventually found Pam's ward after going through a labyrinth of white-walled corridors.

She did look ill. The bright red-gold curls were pulled back off her face by a white bandage, and bruises on her cheek and temple were turning yellow-purple. One leg was suspended in mid-air in plaster, and Pam was staring straight ahead at nothing, a magazine propped open on her lap.

'Lori . . .' She stared at her for a moment, then put a hand to her temple, wincing. 'Sit down. I'm so sorry about this.'

Lorel sat down beside the bed, smiling at her. 'Don't be silly,' she said gently. 'It wasn't your fault.'

Pam sighed, mouth compressing. 'I should have told the doctor. I knew it was appendicitis . . . I just couldn't bear the thought of the operation.'

'That's what I told Robert. I said, "Pam hates hospitals." '

Pam smiled, blue eyes wry. 'You know me so well.'

There was a silence, then Lori asked quietly, 'How do you feel?'

Pam closed her eyes. 'Awful . . . I ache all over.' Her voice was husky, and her face white and drained. 'Every time I try to eat I feel sick.'

A nurse wheeled a trolley past, casting a brisk and efficient eye over them as tin implements on her tray rattled.

'Can I bring you anything?'

Pam swallowed and said throatily, 'Robert's in charge of that.' Her eyes slid to Lorel's face, 'How are the twins?'

'Absolutely adorable,' Lorel said gently.

A smile touched Pam's mouth and she murmured, 'Poor little mites . . .' Leaning back against the pillows, she closed her eyes and Lorel watched her with concern, seeing just how shaken and exhausted she really was. She needed a lot of rest. Lorel decided to make this visit a short one, and stopped in at the Sister's office on her way out to discover exactly what Pam's condition was. Stable, the Sister informed her with a poker-face. Stable, and as well as could be expected.

When she got home, she found Robert watching television in the living-room, and the inane canned laughter floated through the open door as Lorel passed it on her way to the kitchen to make some coffee. The twins were asleep, and after she'd hung her coat up, she popped up to see them.

Robert looked up as she went into the living-room. 'How did it go?'

'Fine.' Lorel relaxed into the big, flowered armchair and kicked off her shoes, leaning back. 'I expected her to be a lot worse than she was. She's tired and bruised, and too dazed to say very much. But she does look as though she'll get better.'

Robert sighed. 'Poor Pammie-Bear.'

'Yes,' she agreed quietly, 'poor Pammie-Bear.'

The television erupted into laughter as a hypnotist got a man to take off his shoes and socks every time someone said the word 'Bingo'.

'I hear you had visitor today,' Robert said quietly, and Lorel froze, staring at him in stunned surprise.

'I . . . meant to tell you,' she said huskily, putting down her cup with fingers that trembled because the mention of Steve Kennedy's visit had hit her like an electric shock, making every nerve-ending come alive.

'The twins can't keep a secret for longer than five minutes,' he said ironically. 'You don't have to tell me who he is. Just ask him not to terrify my kids again.'

Lorel flushed, eyes darting to his. 'I'm sorry . . .'

'No need to be,' Robert replied. 'The way the twins saw it—he was a big bully and you got bullied. Is that right?'

She lowered her lashes. 'That's reasonably accurate.'

He watched her, studying the pale, vulnerable curve of her cheek. 'He's not real trouble, is he? You know you can always turn to me if you need help.'

'Oh, no, nothing like that . . .' She cleared her throat, forcing her voice to remain steady. 'He's the screenwriter. He came down to find out why I wasn't going to Cairo this morning with the rest of the film crew.'

Robert watched her in silence for a moment. Then he said softly, 'Cairo . . . God, I'm sorry, Lorel. That must have meant an awful lot to you. How are we ever going to make it up to you?'

'You don't have to,' she said brightly, eager to get off the subject of Steve's visit today. 'That's what he came down to tell me. They're going to shoot around me. I've still got the part.'

He whistled. 'You must have an angel perched on your shoulder. Can I borrow him? I think mine's a gargoyle!'

She laughed, and started talking about the film, glad to have moved so far away from the subject of Steve Kennedy.

But he remained firmly entrenched in her mind, and when she went to bed that night she found herself lying awake, staring at the back of her eyelids intently as she remembered the way he'd pinned her to Robert and Pam's bed this morning. What disturbed her most was that in her mind's eye she found herself imagining a kiss from him, and the more she tried to stop herself, the stronger the image became. That hard mouth and those long hands . . . she twisted restlessly, hating herself, wishing she could stop her mind betraying her.

Next day, she drove past the White Swan twice, her eyes scanning the car park, but there was no sign of his car, and her heart twisted as she realised he must have left town. Without even saying goodbye. Her mouth tightened. Why should she care where he was or who he was with?

He was probably with that blonde she had seen him getting out of the car with the other night. What a beauty she was! How could Lorel ever compete? Black mink coat and elegant face—Steve Kennedy's kind of woman.

The days passed slowly, and gradually she found herself slipping into a comfortable routine as a temporary housewife. Cooking and cleaning became her pastimes, and she spent a lot of time playing with the twins when they weren't at school. They had bright, lively minds, and made good companions while Robert was at work.

Pam slowly began to recover, and towards the end of the week was actually becoming reasonably talkative. Lorel began to look forward to going to Cairo, sure now that it was only a matter of weeks away.

CHAPTER FIVE

A WEEK after the accident, Lorel visited Pam in hospital, taking a bunch of grapes and the latest Kate Bush album on tape. She'd spent the morning delivering the twins to the playgroup, which was almost a full-time occupation as they always got over-excited. Driving out of the village, she had passed the White Swan and yet again found herself searching the cobbled courtyard for Steve's car. It was absurd, irrational. He had gone and she knew it. He hadn't contacted her, hadn't even left a note. Yet still, every time she passed that damned inn, her eyes darted restlessly along the rows of cars, knowing full well that the long, sleek black Jaguar would not be there. He must have gone back to London, or possibly Cairo. He was an important part of that film; what else did she expect? Yet as she arrived at the hospital and walked along the sterile, squeaky corridors, she felt down and depressed.

Pam, however, was in fine spirits, sitting up in bed dressed in an antique gold-green 1920s négligé set, her heart-shaped face positively glowing with radiance.

Lorel pulled up a chair and studied her. 'I see you're on the road to recovery!'

Pam laughed. 'I've never felt so pampered! Look

at all these presents!'

Lorel glanced at the overflowing bedside table, with chocolates, flowers, cards and gifts. There were cuts and bruises on Pam's face, her cheekbone a livid yellow-purple. Bandages showed through her night-dress, and her fingers were in splints. But considering what she had been through—Pam looked very well.

'Have you seen my leg?' Pam pointed to the plastered leg suspended in mid-air. 'I'm collecting signatures. I insist you sign it.'

'Love to!' Lorel took the pen from the table and went over to her leg.

'It's so cumbersome!' Pam sighed. 'I feel like Long John Silver.'

'Don't worry, I'll buy you a parrot.'

'Not that old chestnut!' Pam groaned. 'If I've heard it once, I've heard it a thousand times. Even your friend Steve Kennedy said it this morning.'

Lorel dropped the pen with a clatter, staring at her sister.

'Steve?' she said hoarsely. 'He was here?'

Pam nodded. 'He told me not to tell you.'

'I'll bet he did!' Lorel said under her breath.

Pam watched her closely, blue eyes narrowed. 'Yes, he did say you'd be cross.'

Hot colour flooded her face. 'I'm not cross!' She dived under the bed to retrieve her pen, needing a few seconds to recover from the shock. What had he been up to? Her heart was thumping madly and she could scarcely believe it was true.

'Oh?' Pam studied her coolly. 'Then why are you hiding under the bed?'

'I'm getting my pen!' Lorel stood up too fast and banged her head sharply on the metal underside of the bed, clutching her cranium and gritting her teeth as tears of pain sprang to her eyes.

'Interesting,' said Pam. 'Why does his name cause such chaos, I wonder?'

'It's not chaos,' Lorel said quickly, sitting down and keeping her eyes as steady as possible. 'I'm just rather puzzled. He had no need to come and visit you. It's absurd.'

'I was rather surprised,' Pam agreed. 'He said he was working with you on the film. Is that true?'

Lorel nodded. 'He's the screenwriter. But even so . . . to come and visit you? I don't know what he was thinking of!'

'You?' suggested Pam coolly.

Her face ran with scarlet colour. 'He's just a friend.'

'Not a boyfriend, then?' Pam watched her with beady eyes.

'No!'

She laughed. 'You said that far too quickly, little sister!'

'I've only known him for a few weeks,' Lorel lied, averting her face.

'How very odd,' drawled Pam. 'He told me you'd known each other five years.'

Lorel lifted her head, her eyes guilty.

'What conflicting stories.' said Pam with a great deal of satisfaction. 'I wonder which one of you is lying?'

Lorel studied her warily. 'What else did he say?'

'Nothing much.' Pam was frowning at her, munching a grape. 'To be honest, I still can't think why he came to see me. I was very surprised when he arrived, and I only let him stay because he bought me such fabulous roses!'

Lorel looked at the enormous bunch of scarlet roses on Pam's bedside table and her mouth tightened. 'I'd like to slap his face!'

Pam's eyes widened. 'How very violent of you! Do you fancy him or something? I must admit, he is wildly attractive. The dominant type, I think.' She contemplated this, popping another grape in her mouth. 'A tough face. But very charming.' She laughed. 'I must say, he does have his moments. He almost made Sister Haversham swoon, and that takes some doing, believe me!'

Lorel said quickly, 'I spoke to her on the way in. She tells me you'll be home within a fortnight.'

Pam brightened. 'Did she?' she said, and began to eagerly discuss what she would do when she was eventually allowed home.

Lorel breathed a sigh of relief, glad to have switched the subject away from Steve Kennedy. Damn him to hell! How dared he come and visit her sister in hospital? If it weren't for Pam's cheerful mood and teasing remarks, Lorel might even have believed Steve had come specifically to ask her about Robert. That would have been the final straw. And she knew Steve was probably capable of anything. He was fearless. She could really grow to hate him.

After leaving the hospital, Lorel went straight to the playgroup where the twins were running riot, showing off as Lorel spoke to Mrs Barleycorn, their teacher.

'Oh, I am glad!' Mrs Barleycorn smiled when Lorel told her Pam was feeling better. 'It's no fun being in hospital, is it? I remember when I was in with my slipped disc; I just didn't know what to do with myself!' She broke off as Billy threw a soft toy at Babs, making her scream with rage. 'Billy, stop that at once! Or you won't be the angel in the nativity!'

Billy immediately behaved, looking angelic.

Lorel dragged them both outside in their matching coats and stuffed them in the back of the car. By the time they got home, they were squabbling violently and pinching each other.

Lorel bundled them inside and started peeling the potatoes and carrots for dinner. Six o'clock came and went, and Lorel tried to keep the dinner from burning, wondering where on earth Robert was.

The twins grew fractious and a fight broke out in the hall. Babs came running in, red in the face with rage, complaining that Billy had torn her doll's head off. Lorel sorted the argument out, threatening to tell their father if they didn't shut up and behave, then went back to the kitchen to find the potatoes slowly falling apart in the saucepan.

At six-forty, the front door opened.

'Your dinner's ruined!' Lorel called out, and started straining the potatoes, although they were by now soggy.

'Sorry, love!' Robert shouted from the front door. 'I got held up.'

His footsteps approached the kitchen. 'Did you have a good day at the office?' Lorel asked.

'Yes, dear!' drawled a horribly familiar voice.

Lorel caught her breath, spinning to see Steve Kennedy lounging in the kitchen doorway looking a million sexy dollars in a black evening suit, cool and composed from the top of his arrogant black head right down the length of that hard body to his shiny black shoes.

'How did you get in?' she demanded breathlessly, heart pounding convulsively at the sight of him.

'I bumped into Robert,' he drawled softly, and the blue eyes glittered with a mocking triumph as he called over one shoulder, 'Didn't I, Robert?'

'We stopped off at the Three Bells for a pint!' Robert came in, rubbing his hands together and sniffing the air. 'Mmm! That smells good! What is it—chicken?'

Lorel barely heard; she was staring at Steve, hating the hard lines of mockery on his face.

'Oh, goody!' drawled Steve sardonically. 'Roast chicken!'

Her mouth tightened. 'There's not enough for you!'

He laughed and murmured teasingly, 'But it's my favourite!'

'Too bad!' she said tightly.

Robert turned his head and gave her a reproving look. 'I'm sure we can stretch to just one more person?'

'And I'm sure we can't!' Lorel snapped, breathing hard as she looked at Steve and hated him more powerfully than she had ever hated anyone in her life before. 'Excuse me please, Robert!' she said, flushing a little, 'I'd like a word with Mr Kennedy in private.'

Lorel pushed him out into the hall and closed the door firmly behind them so that Robert could not hear what was being said.

'What are you doing here?' Her voice was low and angry. 'I thought you'd driven back to London.'

He frowned. 'Why should you think that?'

'Because your car wasn't outside the . . .' she broke off, flushing hotly as she realised she'd given herself away.

The clever blue eyes probed her face. 'I see,' he murmured. 'You checked up on me at the Swan, I suppose? How interesting.'

Her flush deepened and she said defensively, 'I don't like you staying here. It makes me nervous.'

'Does it?' A mocking smile touched the hard mouth. 'Even more interesting! I thought I only got through to you when I lost my temper. Nice to know I have a deeper effect on you than that!'

She was suddenly aware of the proximity of his hard, masculine body, so attractive in the black evening suit, and she could smell the fresh scent of his skin, cold from the November evening outside and glowing with health.

Steve watched her. 'I saw your sister today. I went to the hospital.'

'I know!' Lorel looked up bitterly. 'She told me all about it!'

He laughed. 'And she promised not to!'

'You had no right to do that,' she said in an angry voice. 'She's still weak.'

'I thought she looked rather gorgeous,' he drawled. 'All things considered.'

Dark jealousy flashed in her eyes and she struggled to keep her temper. 'Yes—I heard you flirted with her!'

He grinned. 'Shamelessly!' The blue eyes flickered over her face, lingering on her angry mouth. 'Why? Does that bother you?'

'Of course it doesn't!' she lied, flushing. 'She's a happily married woman. You wouldn't stand a chance with her!'

'My conclusion exactly,' he told her coolly. 'That's what I went there to find out. It only took five minutes to see she wasn't the kind of woman who would tolerate any kind of encroachment on her territory.'

Her eyes held his intensely. 'You didn't mention me? Or Robert?'

'Oh, come on! You don't seriously imagine I'd walk up to a perfect stranger and ask that kind of question? Leave me some credit for good taste!'

'You were perfectly happy to drop hints about me and you, though, weren't you?' she challenged angrily. 'You deliberately gave her the idea that we were . . .' she broke off, her face flooding with colour.

Steve watched her in cool silence for a moment before saying in a deep voice, 'Lovers? Yes, you're right. Your sister thinks I'm your lover.' His eyes mocked her as he said softly, 'She's not far wrong

. . . is she, Lorel?'

She stared at him bitterly. 'What happened between us five years ago was a moment of madness! I was drunk. I was unhappy!' Her eyes flared and she flung hoarsely, 'Why can't you understand that and leave me alone?'

Steve stared, oddly shocked, and she turned away from those searing blue eyes, covering her face with her hands as the hot tears spilled over her lashes. If only there was some way out of this.

'Lorel . . .' His voice was deep as his hands slid softly on to her shoulders. 'Don't . . .'

She shook him off, angry. 'Don't what? Don't cry when you've pushed me to my limits? What do you think I'm made of?'

He drew in his breath, hands tightening on her shoulders. 'I didn't know you had limits. I thought you were indifferent to me.'

'Indifferent?' Turning, she stared at him angrily. 'You've never given me the chance! You're at me constantly. Taunting me, hurting me—reminding me what a stupid little fool I was! Can't you accept that I just wanted to forget you?'

His mouth hardened. 'No, I damned well can't,' he said under his breath. 'I have limits, too. Has it ever occurred to you that I didn't want to forget you? That I couldn't get you out of my mind?'

Lorel went very still. 'Oh?' Her voice was husky, and she was suddenly intensely aware of those long hands on her shoulders. 'Why couldn't you get me out of your mind?'

He was silent for a moment, then said coolly, 'You

were different. Oddly vulnerable—a hurt little girl more than a woman.' His mouth twisted. 'I found you refreshing. My usual brand of woman is sophisticated, elegant, sure of herself. I'm sure you know the type.'

'Man-eaters.'

'Red talons and mink coats,' he drawled. 'I was sick to death of them when I arrived at your sister's wedding. I'd just narrowly escaped marrying one of them. A particularly vicious lady who was only after my money and status.'

Lorel looked up through her lashes. 'Don't tell me she didn't find you attractive, too!'

He smiled slowly and murmured, 'You think so?'

Her heart skipped a beat at the look in his eyes. 'I don't see why not,' she said, oddly breathless.

His hands slid slowly to her waist and he bent his head until his hard mouth was very close to hers. 'And you? Do you find me attractive?'

'I . . .' Her mouth went dry and she said huskily, 'You're quite good-looking.'

He laughed against her mouth and she felt his warm breath fan her skin, making her heart thud even faster as she stood totally still, unwilling to move away from his hard body.

'I'm flattered,' he drawled. 'You always treat me as an enemy.'

'And so you are!' she said huskily. 'All you ever do is insult and bully me. Can't we ever have a civilised conversation?'

There was a peculiar stillness as he said, 'Would you like that?'

She nodded. 'Of course. Anything would be better than this constant round of accusations.'

He watched her through half-closed lids, the blue eyes gleaming. 'How does dinner for two sound?'

Lorel met his gaze, her pulses thudding as she nodded once, jerkily.

'Good.' His mouth hardened with triumph. 'Get your coat. I've already booked a table for seven-thirty.'

The speed of his decision left her reeling. 'But I can't . . . what about Robert? The twins? I've cooked——'

'Robert was planning to take the twins with him to see Pamela,' Steve told her coolly. 'You've got the night off.'

She studied him carefully and said, 'You arranged all this with Robert, before you got here. Didn't you?'

His brows lifted coldly. 'Is that a crime?'

Dumbly, she shook her head. The idea of having dinner with him was strangely attractive.

Steve watched her, eyes narrowing on her mouth. Then suddenly his head bent before she could back off, and his mouth caught hers hotly, making her shudder with fierce pleasure.

'Get your coat,' he said, an odd huskiness in his voice, and then he was gone, the kitchen door swinging shut behind him as he went to speak to Robert, leaving Lorel staring at nothing, her fingers shakily retracing the outline of his mouth on hers.

Later, as they drove to Laysham, she glanced across

at him through her lashes in the silver-grey luxury of the darkened car. It gave her a strange pleasure to sit here with him in silence, watching him drive, his long, tanned hands firm on the wheel, flicking the main beam headlight off when another car passed, then back on with a cool touch of his finger. Driving was such a masculine skill, and Steve had such control, his eyes coolly narrowed on the road ahead, lashes flickering momentarily as he glanced in the rear-view mirror.

He caught her looking at him, and a smile touched the hard mouth. 'Something interesting you?' he drawled.

She lowered her lashes, colouring a little, and they drove on in silence. On the outskirts of town, he signalled right and Lorel looked up through the rain in alarm.

'Oh, no!' She sat forward, staring at the wet sign swinging in the rain above white stone gates and thick hedgerows. 'Not here!'

Steve shot her an oblique look. 'I thought it appropriate,' he drawled coolly, and turned right.

She stared in horror as they swung through the tall stone gates, up the long, wet, tree-lined drive to the Manor House Hotel.

The tall, white house came into view and her mouth went dry, leaving her reeling with memories of her sister's wedding, of she and Steve standing on those stone steps arguing, and of Steve catching her when she lost consciousness.

'I don't want to eat here!'

There was the mermaid fountain, the long-haired

lady sitting on her rock with a cold bronze smile while water cascaded around her. There was the long, rose-trellised garden far in the outer corners of the estate, where Steve had overhead her passionate exchange with Robert.

'Please . . .' Lorel's hand instinctively clutched his arm as he parked in the cobbled courtyard, 'let's go somewhere else.'

He switched off the engine. 'You haven't been here,' he asked deeply, turning, 'since that night?'

Lorel bent her red-gold head and said shakily, 'I left town soon afterwards. Drama School started that autumn and I was lucky to get a place. I took it with both hands.'

He watched her, his eyes catlike. 'Then it'll be something of an experience for us both,' he said softly. 'Won't it?'

He got out and came round to her side, opening the door, taking her arm and pulling her to her feet, scrutinising her white, frightened face.

'It's only bricks and mortar,' he said deeply. 'It can't hurt you.'

'Then why bring me here? There are plenty of other places to go!'

'I was interested in your reaction,' he drawled. 'And so far, it's been very informative!' His eyes mocked her and she felt a flare of anger.

'I could hate you!' she said under her breath.

He laughed and took her hand, pulling her away from the shade of the eucalyptus trees and across the cobbled courtyard, past the mermaid and towards the steps. Lorel shivered, pulling her camelhair coat closer.

Her heels rang out on the stone steps as she ascended beside Steve. Her gold ear-rings glittered under the lights, her face free from make-up save for a smudge of lipstick.

Inside it was warm and filled with voices, people moving from the lifts as they emptied, rang and zoomed up again.

Lorel stood beside Steve, staring. It had barely changed in five years. Oh, there was a new coat of paint, and new creamy-gold wallpaper. A Jazz Age gilt-edged mirror on the wall opposite them, and a new set of oil paintings scattered on the walls. But, apart from that, it was almost untouched.

It was as though time had stood still.

'May I take your coats?' A black-jacketed waiter swept up to them. 'Your name, sir?'

'Kennedy.' He shrugged off the black cashmere coat and white silk scarf. 'I have a table booked for seven-thirty.'

Lorel handed her coat over and a wave of expensive scent enveloped her, lifting from her wrists and throat in a soft warm cloud. Her red-gold hair spilling freshly over her shoulders was a good contrast with the blue woollen dress.

'Nice scent . . .' drawled Steve discreetly, as they went into the Art Nouveau dining-room with its palms and pillars and mirrors and an air of the Jazz Age. 'What is it?'

'Chanel.' Lorel sat down at the table, the pink damask tablecloth gleaming with silver, a single pink rose in a fluted silver vase, and a soft golden haze from the lighting.

'No. 5?' Steve smiled lazily. 'Monroe wore nothing else in bed.'

She gave him a frosty look. 'I am not Monroe.'

'No,' he murmured, one long finger resting on his hard mouth as he scrutinised her, 'but you do have a certain vulnerability that gives you . . . shall we say, a little mystery?'

She lowered her lashes. 'I'd hoped it didn't show.' she said huskily. 'We all try to disguise our weaknesses.'

'And what are your weaknesses?' he asked coolly.

Lorel dimpled. 'Dover sole with salad,' she said deliberately, and bent her eyes to the gilt-embossed menu, thus ending the discussion.

Steve laughed softly. 'Cheat!'

True to her word, Lorel chose Dover sole with salad for her main course, with melon to start. If she was going to be filming for the foreseeable future, she would have to keep a strict eye on her figure. Celluloid preferred bones to flesh, and she had no wish to lose her chance of success simply for the sake of a portion of chips. She sighed, resigning herself to a life of purity and denial, and decided it would be truly wonderful if it suddenly became fashionable to be a little plumper, rather than constantly starving oneself into a beanpole shape.

'How did you manage to talk Robert into bringing you home?' Lorel asked as they ate their main course a little while later.

Steve looked up through thick lashes. 'Quite simple, really,' he drawled, pouring some more wine.

'I called him into the Senior Partner's office and laid my cards on the table. Once he knew who I was and why I was here, it was a simple matter of a couple of pints in the Three Bells and then back to his place.'

Lorel frowned. 'I take it you know the Senior Partner?'

Steve's eyes gleamed. 'He happens to be my cousin.'

'Howard Jefferson is your cousin?' Lorel's mouth dropped open with surprise. 'But I know him!' He was a tall, dynamic man with a ferocious sense of humour and a great deal of verve, who had put a rocket under Robert's accountancy firm seven years ago and turned it into a thriving part of his own accountancy firm, further afield in Bath.

'I have a large family,' Steve drawled, sipping wine. 'We have tentacles everywhere!'

'I always picture you as an only child . . .' Lorel said faintly, studying him. 'Probably because you strike me as spoilt!'

'Far from it!' He laughed. 'I had to fight for my share of attention with five other kids.'

Lorel's eyes widened. 'Five!'

'I loathed them all until I was about thirty,' he said wryly. 'About the same time I met you, in fact. The competition in the family was fierce, believe me. We all hated each other like poison and used to gloat over various mistakes we made when we finally all flew the nest.'

'I only ever had Pam,' Lorel said with a slight smile, 'and we always got on well. But then she's nearly the same age as me, and we were . . . friends,

I suppose, when we were children. That kind of bonding doesn't die easily.'

'Nor does competition, let me tell you,' he drawled, eyes glittering with amusement. 'When my elder sister landed a job in television I nearly foamed at the mouth! I was jealous and angry, and we didn't speak to each other for two years, except for the odd snarl at Christmas over the family dinner-table.' He laughed. 'Of course, time mellowed me. When I found success of my own, I was able to accept hers with a little more grace.'

Lorel was astonished at this totally new portrait of Steve, struggling for recognition in a large family of achievers.

'What does she do in television?'

'Geraldine?' he smiled. 'She used to direct a lot of plays—you know the type of thing, BBC plays. But she doesn't work very often these days. Too busy raising her own family.'

'Oh . . .' Lorel smiled. 'But surely television shouldn't have threatened you? You were in films —that's a different medium entirely.'

'I wasn't in films, though,' he said drily. 'I was out of work and out of luck. I had no money, no future and just wrote feverishly all day long in the hope of flogging my work to someone. I was only twenty at the time. Geraldine was already twenty-eight.'

'Are you the youngest?'

He shook his dark head. 'A middle child. The eldest son. I have two elder sisters and three younger brothers.'

'I can't imagine a family that big.' Lorel studied

him with new eyes, picturing him with all those brothers and sisters, all vying for attention in what must have been an uproarious household. 'It sounds like something out of a psychologist's nightmare!'

'It was, believe me,' Steve drawled coolly. 'I had my work cut out forging a strong identity. We all did. But maybe that's why we're so successful in our own fields. We had to be, you see.'

She leaned forwards, fascinated, her slender hand playing with the stem of her glass. 'What do the others do?'

'Various money-making enterprises.' He lifted the claret to his lips and drank lazily. 'My sister Kathleen runs a model agency. Michael's a top-flight lawyer. Patrick's in banking and Edward's a music business impresario.'

Lorel studied him, her gaze skimming the hard face. What must it have been like to grow up in that family? Steve was a success in his own right, with a string of major international films behind him and already one Oscar to his credit. But even so, it couldn't have been easy with that kind of sibling rivalry.

'Tell me about your parents,' she said suddenly.

He laughed softly, eyes meeting hers. 'Playing psychiatrist? Shall I get on the couch?'

She smiled, looking at him through her lashes. 'Why not?'

His gaze dropped to her mouth. 'Only if you come with me.'

Lorel flushed, bending her head. Her pulses skipped every time that dark voice lowered, every time she felt his eyes on her, burning in that intent way, as though he was about to make love to her.

'My mother's adorable,' Steve said after a moment's silence. 'An Irish redhead, full of fire but elegant with it. The kind of woman who can walk about in bare feet and still look like a duchess instead of a peasant.'

Lorel's eyes widened. 'I pictured her as dark-haired.'

He shook his head. 'That's my father. He's English—very English. Educated at Oxford and with a sharp business sense. Rich and very, very clever.'

Lorel tilted her head to one side and said slowly, 'Why are people always so differnet from the way we imagine them?'

'That's part of the fun, though, isn't it?' His smile was lazy, seductive. 'It gives life an edge over other, more predictable hobbies.'

She laughed, green eyes glittering. 'The game of life?'

'Quite so,' he drawled. 'You throw first.'

After dinner, as they left the restaurant, Lorel was surprised to see Steve turn left when he should have turned right. She followed him quickly, catching his sleeve as he strode ahead of her along the palm-lined corridor of gilt-edged mirrors.

'The exit is this way.'

He looked at her oddly. 'I'm just curious to see how the hotel has changed. Aren't you?'

She felt a shiver of alarm. 'No. I want to go home.'

His mouth crooked in a sardonic smile. 'Don't be

a party-pooper,' he drawled, taking her hand. Those long fingers closed tightly over her wrist, leading her into the ballroom.

Lorel allowed herself to be pulled, her pulses thudding and her hand suddenly clinging on to his as though she felt suddenly unsafe. She did. Very unsafe.

The tall, white-gold pillars and glittering chandeliers were exactly the same; the palms and fresh-cut roses filled the room with a clean, pure scent. The polished wood floor echoed under her feet, and the long Twenties mirrors reflected gold light in a soft sheen.

'It seems so . . . empty.' Her voice echoed softly.

He nodded. 'Can't you hear the ghosts?' He looked around, memories in the blue eyes, and said softly, 'That god-awful band your father hired . . . and when everyone had gone, the way you still danced like a gypsy in the centre of it all. Only a few stray guests still watching with drinks in their hands . . .'

'Ugh!' Lorel made a face. 'I don't really want to remember it all.'

'Why not?' He turned, his brows drawn in a slight frown. 'What's so wrong about having a good time when you're young? That's all you were doing, Lorelei.'

She sighed and said huskily, 'Can we go now?'

Steve looked at her for a long moment, then nodded. 'Sure.'

But as they passed the lifts, he suddenly stopped and seemed to consider something for a long moment, before walking towards the lifts and jabbing the call button with one long finger.

'I am not going upstairs!' Lorel hissed in her ear as the lift arrived and a middle-aged couple stepped out, a wave of cloying scent drifting from the woman.

'It'll only be for a moment,' Steve assured her, dragging her into the lift against her will. 'I just want to see the upstairs . . . see if it's changed.'

'Look!' Lorel was alarmed by now, and her heartbeat sped up alarmingly. 'I don't want to take a trip down memory lane. Can't you understand that? I want to forget it all!'

He pressed button seven and the lift zoomed upwards.

'This is stupid!' Lorel said shakily as Steve led her along the corridor to the seventh floor.

She did not recognise any of it. Not one inch of carpet, not one creamy-gold door. It could have been any hotel corridor in the world. Yet with Steve Kennedy beside her it took on new meaning, gave her a deeper sense of intimacy with him, made her feel both excited and afraid and unwilling to chart this territory.

'Suite 707 . . .' Steve said huskily as they stopped outside the door, and Lorel pulled back, feeling nauseous as she saw the creamy-gold door with gilt letters.

She heard the key jangle in his pocket, saw him take it out and insert it in the lock.

'Oh, God . . .'

Her heartbeat thudded like a racehorse at the finishing post as the door swung open and she was catapulated back in time to the moment when she lost her innocence in the dark, satanic fever of a stranger's arms . . .

CHAPTER SIX

THERE was the pale green and gold brocade bed, the tall, mirrored wardrobes with their ornate gold handles, the long, heavy, pale green-gold curtains roped in the centre like thin-waisted ladies, with tasselled sashes. The carpet was soft under her feet, pale green and almost silky-smooth. A gold eighteenth-century carriage clock on the mantelpiece, a writing-desk with leather desk set, and an intricately carved creamy-gold dressing-table with three mirrors and a tiny Art Nouveau lamp at the side in gold and white.

Lorel was barely able to breathe as she looked around the room. It was so pretty, so antique, so tastefully decorated. How could she have thought it sordid five years ago? Such style and understated wealth could never be sordid.

The door closed behind them and she whirled, heart in her mouth, to face Steve.

He leant against the white-gold door, watching her silently through those thick black lashes, and she dared not move or breathe or speak, simply stared at him, feeling that sense of intimacy deepen to a level inside them both that frightened her.

Seconds passed as they looked at one another across that gold and silent room, everything in their own worlds stripping away, suddenly irrelevant.

He seemed to her to be the one real thing in life, and the shock of that realisation made her alarm deeper, for she knew at that moment that she was in love with him, and the realisation made her feel sick and afraid for herself.

'You planned this?' she asked huskily, eventually.

Steve replied, 'I didn't know until the last moment whether or not I'd actually bring you here.'

Lorel nodded jerkily, her body taut. 'What made you decide?'

He studied her intently. 'Your fear.'

She laughed with tense gaiety. 'How clever of you!'

He did not move. 'And you're still afraid.'

'Of a room?' She gave him a brilliant, fragile smile. 'Of a bed?'

'I doubt it.'

'Then how silly!' she said in a brittle and enchanting voice. 'And I am pleased—really, I am! I was curious about Suite 707, I must admit. But now that I've seen it, I know there's nothing here but a ghost, a bed and a stranger.'

He watched her with dark, dark eyes.

Lorel walked up to him, her body as tight as a bow-string. 'Shall we go? It's getting late and Robert will be worried——'

'You're nervous,' he said softly. 'Don't be . . .'

'I mean, I'm very grateful to you for bringing me here. I've had a lovely time, but I really would like to go home now . . .'

'Lorel, I didn't make love to you,' he said softly,

and time seemed to stand still as the words left his lips.

Lorel stared at him for what seemed an eternity, each word etching itself into her mind with each stroke of the carriage clock, chiming in the background.

'I brought you up here to tell you that,' Steve said on the last stroke of midnight. 'I've been meaning to tell you for a long time. But I had to pick my moment, and it never seemed right until now.'

'Nothing happened?' she whispered. 'Nothing at all?'

'Nothing at all.' His mouth moved in a smile. 'Though God knows I wanted more . . . you were so lovely . . . eighteen, ravishing, and lying naked on that bed . . . how I restrained myself, I still don't know! When you put your arms around my neck and pulled me down on top of you, I lost control for a second. I wanted to make love to you like crazy . . . but I just couldn't bring myself to do it. Not when you were so obviously drunk. You didn't know what you were doing, and I did.' He gave a broad shrug, smiling. 'So I stole a very tempting kiss . . . looked you up and down with absolute longing . . .' he laughed softly and finished, 'and then turned over and went to sleep! My God, I deserve an award!'

Lorel could barely speak or breathe, but managed to say huskily, 'You didn't . . . touch me?'

He shook his head, and his eyes darkened. 'I wanted to. Believe me, I almost went crazy trying to stop myself. Your seduction technique is mindbending, and I had a lot of trouble keeping the upper hand! Talk about a power struggle! But I didn't touch you. Not unless you count putting my arms around you and holding you very close indeed. But then . . .' he smiled crookedly, 'I think I can be forgiven that one lapse.'

Her eyes flicked from his to the wall, staring unseeingly as she felt herself fill up with conflicting emotions.

She was free. She was innocent. Relief flooded over her and she felt the years of self-hatred and fear peel away from her like seven veils in a long, slow dance. It hadn't happened! None of it!

Anger took over and her lips whitened as she looked back over her life and saw it as an emotional wasteland. I shut myself away, she thought, because I thought I was too reckless, too foolish to be trusted again. And I'd done nothing! Nothing!

'Well?' Steve was watching her with a smile. 'Are you pleased?'

'Pleased?' She stared at him as though he were mad, then slapped him hard.

His head jerked back, eyes stunned and angry. 'What was that for?'

'For ruining my life!' she flung bitterly. 'For lying to me . . . making me believe I'd gone to bed with a stranger. I've spent the last five years hating myself for something that never even happened, and you expect me to be pleased. Pleased!'

He stared at her, shaken. 'I didn't know . . . I didn't think . . .'

'I feel as though I've been in limbo for years . . .' She ran a trembling hand through her red-gold hair.

'No love, no relationships . . . I didn't dare go near men in case I let myself down again. I couldn't bring myself to trust, to even think of loving . . .'

'But you forgot it all,' Steve said huskily. 'You told me so yourself . . .'

'Yes, I forgot it,' she said, closing her eyes. 'I forgot the wedding night, the alcohol, the way I collapsed. I forgot you and I forgot the kiss and I forgot waking up naked beside you . . .' She turned to look at him, bitterness in her eyes. 'But I never forgot that feeling . . . that sick self-hatred. Like a dirty smudge on my life, waiting to smudge itself all over me again if I ever let a man too close!'

He stared at her in shock silence, the blue eyes reflecting the hurt in hers.

'Can you give me back those years?' Lorel asked in a low, angry voice. 'Can you wave a magic wand and make me eighteen again?'

His mouth tightened and he looked away. 'No one can . . . I'm sorry.'

'Sorry!' Her mouth shook with rage. 'You selfish bastard—you've ruined my life and . . .'

'Now just a minute!' he said angrily. 'This isn't entirely my fault! You should have woken me up and asked me if you were so worried about it——'

'I couldn't,' she said flatly. 'I just wanted to get out of the room.'

'Then don't blame me for what happened!' he replied. 'You had every chance to come back the next day and ask me about it. You didn't have to spend five years not knowing whether or not you'd fallen into bed with me.'

'And you didn't have to lie to me when you made your reappearance!'

He looked away, a faint trace of red along his cheekbones. 'I was hurt,' he said deeply. 'My pride was hurt . . . my ego . . .'

'Your pride!' she said with loathing. 'Your ego!'

'Don't be so quick to judge me!' he said in a low voice, looking at her through his lashes, a muscle jerking in his cheek. 'You might have done the same in my position.'

'I seriously doubt it!' she said scathingly.

'You don't know until it happens to you. Or haven't you learnt that yet? No, I don't suppose you have. You made one mistake and steered clear of men for the rest of your life. Too scared to risk it again, weren't you?' His mouth tightened angrily. 'Well, I may be selfish and ruthless, Lorel, but at least I'm still out there fighting. And if I'm wounded, then I kick back with everything I've got!'

'No matter who gets hurt?' she said bitterly.

He fell silent, studying her through those long, thick lashes, his face strong and hard. 'I'm thirty-five years old, Lorel, and I know how to survive. It isn't easy, I'll admit, but it's a lot easier once you accept that that's the way the game is played.'

Lorel looked away, heaving a long sigh. He was right and she had to admit it, if not to him then to herself. If she had been in his position, she might well have deliberately tried to hurt. It couldn't have been very pleasant to be forgotten. Yet the truth was, he hadn't been.

The truth, as she knew to her cost, was that she

was in love with him. In love with that hard, driving masculinity, the toughness of his mouth and the fiery emotion in his eyes. The way he walked, so arrogant and self-assured, the way he broke into laughter at a moment's notice, eyes lighting with a strong sense of humour. She loved the quick, dynamic mind, the sudden outbursts of temper and the paradox of tenderness when he realised he had hurt her.

Lorel closed her eyes, sick with excitement and anguish. She was in love for the first time, and her heart blazed brilliant colours, yet she did not trust him. She did not dare.

Men like Steve Kennedy were conquerors. He would demand everything she had, strip her of her love and take her passion hungrily until she was unable to give any more. Then he would grow bored, restless; that dynamic body would pace the floor and his eyes would turn black with resentment if he ever felt caged.

'Lorel . . .' His dark, smoky voice was at her ear, and she jumped, heart thudding. 'Can't we call it quits? Forgive and forget?'

'I . . .' Her mouth was suddenly dry and she swallowed convulsively. 'I need time . . .'

His breath fanned her neck, made her rush with heat, wish she could put her arms around his strong neck and call him her own.

'When you come to Egypt,' he said decisively, 'it'll be neutral territory. No memories, and no ghosts. Maybe there we'll have a chance to get to know each other, without bitterness and preconceptions.'

Lorel nodded shakily, her heart thudding. 'That

THE HEAT IS ON

would be nice . . .' she said huskily, looking at him through her lashes. 'We don't really know much about each other, do we?'

A smile touched the hard mouth. 'Oh, I don't know . . .' he drawled softly, turning her to face him, the blue eyes dark and sexy on her mouth. 'We know this . . .'

The dark head moved slowly downwards, giving her every chance to escape, but she did not move, did not want to move, and her lids fell shut as his hard mouth moved over hers slowly, pushing her lips apart and sliding his tongue between them until she groaned in the back of her throat and put her hands up where they belonged, around his neck, pushing through his black hair and claiming ownership of the dark head and all the power inside it that made him hers, all the restlessness, the strength, the temper and humour and irresistible sex-appeal.

Heart thudding as she heard him groan, felt his hands slide sexily over her stomach and up towards her breasts, Lorel waited with burning hunger to feel his hands touch her, then came to her senses and broke away, her eyes glittering feverishly.

'You're going too fast,' she said breathlessly, hands resting on her broad shoulders. 'I'm not ready . . .'

'OK . . .' he said thickly, his face darkly flushed. 'I can wait.' But she could hear the pace of his heart and knew that his temperature had shot up even higher than hers with that one burning kiss.

As they drove home, she felt tense and restless beside him, casting quick, shadowed glances at his face. She felt as though she were about to explode, her body so strung up that just one touch would send her leaping into those strong arms without a thought; her body now so completely his that all he would have to do was stop the car, reach over, look at her with those dark, dark eyes . . .

The car pulled up outside her brother-in-law's house and she looked at it as if she had never seen it before. She felt alive, new, different, as though reborn by some miracle into a world filled with her own senses and her deep longing for Steve Kennedy, for everything about him, every mood, every word from those hard lips, every touch of those long hands.

'I'm flying to Cairo tomorrow,' Steve told her as they sat in the electrically charged atmosphere inside the darkened car. 'I won't see you before I go.'

Lorel felt a desperate sense of loss and her eyes reflected it. 'Oh . . .' Her lips parted on a sigh.

Steve slid his hand over her face, leaning close. 'It won't be long . . . your sister will be out in a fortnight or so. You can contact me at the Cairo Hilton as soon as you know when you're flying out. I'll pick you up at the airport.'

Lorel nodded, afraid to say more in case she gave her feelings away too much. 'I . . .' she said huskily, 'I'll look forward to it.'

He studied her. 'And I'll miss you.'

Lorel closed her eyes on a wave of feeling and his mouth moved over hers in a lingering goodbye kiss. She touched his hard face, felt the unshaven jaw rough with the day's new growth, and ran her fingers over the hard neck and black hair.

He drew away, his face unreadable.

Lorel fumbled with the door-handle and stepped out into the cold night air, bending to the open window to whisper, 'Goodnight . . .'

'Goodnight, Lorel.' The blue pinpoints of light in his eyes were the last thing she saw as the car slowly drew away, and she stood watching the red tail-lights disappear into the distance.

The days passed slowly at first, and Lorel spent her time daydreaming, a glazed look in her eyes as she pictured Steve in the desert sun, by the Pyramids, driving around Cairo in battered, dusty taxis, working on the film, resting at the Cairo Hilton. She expected to hear from him. A postcard, a phone call—something to let her know he was thinking of her. But nothing came, and after ten days Lorel was pretty certain that nothing would.

Yet to send her something, a postcard or letter, would be an obvious admission of feelings on his part. So, although she was deeply disappointed, she could not blame him for his total silence. And he wouldn't be the man he was if he went around dashing off postcards to her all the time, anyway. Not after such a short period of actually being civilised towards each other. After all—it had only been that one night at the Manor House Hotel that the tide had suddenly chnged, allowing her to see him as a reasonable human being.

At the end of a fortnight, Pam was almost ready for release. By now, she was sitting up in the leisure area playing games, reading and watching television with the other patients.

'Checkmate!' Pam announced triumphantly at the end of the ward.

Lorel grinned, walking quietly over to the glass doors of the day area where Pam sat up in her woolly dressing-gown playing chess with a young man from the adjoining ward.

'I'm afraid not!' said the young man, grinning, and took her queen with his knight. 'In fact, now *you're* in checkmate . . .' His eyes scanned the board and he added wryly, 'With no way out!'

Pam studied the board in a cross silence. 'That's what you think!' she said, and swept all the pieces off the board, clattering to the floor.

The young man gawped. 'You cheat!'

'Moi?' Pam battered her eyelashes at him.

'I've never met such a bad loser!'

'Everyone is a bad loser,' Pam said serenely. 'It's just that some people are better at pretending they don't mind, that's all.'

Lorel stood in the doorway, laughing, and Pam turned her head to look at her.

'Something amusing you?' she asked drily.

Lorel dimpled. 'Shades of childhood.' She looked at the young man, who was surveying the debris with amasement, and said, 'She used to do this all the time. The only way to combat it is to stop playing chess with her.'

'I've got no one else to play with,' said the young man, making a face. 'Everyone in my ward is almost geriatric. All they want to do is read books or tell me about their lives.'

'Well,' Lorel frowned, 'play Monopoly with her. She's good at that. But for God's sake, let her buy Park Lane and Mayfair!'

A moment later, she wheeled Pam out of the day area and back into her own ward, going towards her bed on the shiny black and white linoleum. Pam's bed looked as though Santa had just been, and she had emptied the contents of her Christmas stocking all over the bed. Chocolate boxes, books, a shiny red Walkman, tapes and magazines littered the white blankets.

'Sister keeps harping on about how I must live after my release,' Pam said as Lorel parked her at the bed. 'Honestly! It's going to be so dreary with this stupid leg!'

Lorel studied it. 'It is cumbersome,' she agreed.

'It's all right for you,' Pam said with a sigh. 'You're off to Cairo. Have you rung them yet? Do they know when you're arriving?'

Lorel's pulses skipped and she said huskily, 'I'll ring them this afternoon. When I get back.' She had put it off, almost savouring the moment when she would speak to Steve.

'Well, you'd better get a move on,' Pam frowned. 'It's been over a fortnight since that guy left. Have you heard from him at all?'

Lorel looked away and kept her face cool. 'I didn't expect to.'

Pam studied her shrewdly. 'Didn't you?' Her brows rose. 'I did. He followed you down here, didn't he?'

'Only for professional reasons,' Lorel told her

defensively.

'Oh, yes?' Pam laughed. 'Then why have you gone all pink and prickly like a nasty little hedgehog?'

Lorel was glad to get home and away from Pam's teasing. Tomorrow she would drive her home and collect her cases, once she had made sure that everything would be all right. She didn't want to leave Pam and Robert to cope if it proved impossible. Pam was still weak, and her leg was certainly going to give her problems.

Heart thudding, Lorel picked up the phone. Her finger shook as she dialled the code for Egypt, then Cairo, then the telephone number of the Cairo Hilton.

It took a long time for the line to ring. Lorel waited in a tense silence for the phone to be answered, and when it was, she was astonished to hear a crisp English voice say, 'Good evening. Cairo Hilton.'

Lorel said quickly, 'Mr Steven Kennedy, please.'

'One moment, please.' The receptionist went off the line and the long ringing tone started in Steve's room.

It was picked up on the fifth ring, just when Lorel was giving up hope.

'Yes?' Steve's voice barked down the line and her heart leapt at the dark tones.

'Steve?' her voice echoed down the line, breathless and nervous. 'It's Lorel.'

There was a short silence and she heard him breathing, wondered why he sounded out of breath, as though he had run to answer the phone.

'Hi,' he said coolly. 'How are things over there?'

Lorel moistened her lips. 'Fine!' Silence. 'I—I was ringing to let you know my sister is better. She's coming out of hospital tomorrow.'

'I see.' He sounded so far away. 'When are you flying out to Cairo?'

'Thursday,' Lorel said loudly, her heart thudding. 'I want to see her settled in before I leave.'

'I'll meet your plane. What time does it get in?'

'Nine p.m.,' Lorel called, and fumbled with her typed schedule from the travel agents. 'Flight 790.'

There was a short silence, then he said, 'I'll be there.'

Lorel waited, her mouth dry, then asked hesitantly, 'How are you?'

He laughed. 'Hot!'

Lorel laughed too, nervously. 'Take a shower!'

'I just did,' he drawled distantly. 'I'm standing here with water dripping all over me and nothing but a towel round my waist. And I'm still hot!'

A vivid picture flashed into her mind of him naked but for a towel, lights in his bedroom, and the dark, palm-lined sky outside. If only she were there now.

'I . . .' she began, but Steve cut in coolly.

'I'll see you on Thursday,' he said. 'Goodbye, Lorel.'

She was disappointed, but said, 'Goodbye!' and put the phone down with regret.

CHAPTER SEVEN

HER flight was late, night had fallen, and Cairo Airport was a mad, bustling place of draughty stone rooms, dusty halls, and curling Arabic script in peeling red paint on every wall. Lorel went through passport control with the shuffling throng, picked up her cases and passed through Customs into the outer hall. Egyptian men in shirt-sleeves and black moustaches eyed her slender white body as she passed, and Lorel knew a moment of fear at the looks in their eyes, until she noticed a young Egyptian official watching her, and because of the warmth of his smile, felt immediately comfortable again.

Her green eyes scanned the barrier as she swept through, looking for a sign of Steve's dark head. The tannoy boomed announcements in lyrical Arabic, footsteps and voices echoed around the wide, empty hall.

She saw a card saying Lorelei Lane, and made a bee-line for the tall, gangly young man who held it.

'Hi.' She almost bumped into him as an Egyptian pushed past her. 'I'm Lorelei.'

'I recognised you,' he said, eyeing her white shirt-dress with a smile. 'Kennedy told me to watch out for a girl with red hair and shameless sex appeal.'

'Oh?' She smiled, looking around. 'Where is he?'

'Charging around Cairo on urgent business,' the young man said, picking up her cases. 'He couldn't make it, so he sent me instead.'

Lorel stood totally still as though she had been slapped, staring after the young man who was now walking away from her towards the doors.

'Just a minute . . .' She caught up with him, green eyes anxious. 'How do I know you're with the crew?'

'Who else would have me?' He laughed, looking down at his faded jeans and scruffy white T-shirt.

Lorel stood watching him load the cases into a battered and dusty Fiat while the madness of Cairo went on all around them, taxi drivers shouting and gesturing at each other while cars veered dangerously around corners, Arabic music wailing from their open windows.

'I'm Chris, by the way.' He started the car. 'Chris Goodfellow.'

Lorel swallowed her hurt pride. 'Do you live up to your name?' she asked, trying to forget Steve's let-down.

'Not if I can help it!'

They shot towards the city in a hair-raising drive that took years off her life.

'Don't you just love it?' Chris shouted above the noise as they screeched round the city streets, alive with music and colour and people, Egyptians in western clothes running dangerously across the road, black hair and black moustaches and deep, deep brown skin.

'It's so noisy!' Lorel shouted back, clutching the door-handle as a taxi blasted them out of the way, the driver shaking his fist at them. 'I've never seen anything like it.'

'Wait till you see Luxor!' Chris shouted back as they passed peeling sun-bleached buildings with dusty Arabic script on them in bizarre baked colours. 'It's more dirty and alive and ancient than this place. Cairo is fabulous, but it's a little too civilised for me. Luxor is a place you just fall in love with, believe me.'

Loirel smiled. 'It'll probably scare me to death!'

'Then I'll order your coffin! You're going there on Sunday!'

She stared at him. 'But I thought we were only filming in Cairo!'

'We're all wrapped up here except for your scenes,' Chris told her. 'Once we've shot them, the whole crew is off to Luxor—and that means you!'

Lorel stared at the city lights, and wondered where Steve was and why he hadn't told her they were going to Luxor. Was he going too? Or would he be flying back?

The car pulled up at a crossroads, and Lorel glanced idly to her left into a brightly lit bar where men sat talking, their faces sun-baked, hair black as night, and she wondered what it must be like to live here.

Then she saw them. Steve Kennedy and a blonde woman standing in the centre of the bar arguing across a table, their faces angry, and as she watched Steve slid one strong hand around the woman's wrist, jerking her back as she tried to leave, saying something so bitingly angry that some of the men in the bar turned to watch, their eyes narrowed with interest.

The car was pulling away, but Lorel's eyes were fixed on Steve and the blonde, and she felt a slow, sick jealousy like a knife in her stomach as she watched the woman try to run, only to be pulled back by Steve until her body rested tightly against his, their faces inches apart.

They were out of sight now, and Lorel sat frozen in her seat, unable to speak or breathe because the shock was too much for her to cope with.

'See the Pyramids?' Chris was saying. 'Just above the city? That's where you're filming tomorrow . . .' But she barely heard him.

Was that what had been so urgent . . . a meeting with that blonde woman? That they were involved with each other was obvious, and Lorel felt a strong sense of recognition, as though she'd seen that blonde before somewhere . . .

They were pulling up outside the Cairo Hilton, and she was forced to act normally, make casual conversation with this indifferent stranger whom Steve had sent in his place.

'You're in room 1922,' Chris was saying as he handed her the key at the crowded reception desk. 'I hate to sound boring, but I'd go straight to sleep if I were you.'

Lorel gave a tense smile. 'I'm far too excited,' she said, although she felt nothing but hurt and angry.

'You'll be far too exhausted if you don't,' Chris drawled lightly as they walked to the lifts. 'We start shooting at five tomorrow morning. You have to be in make-up at four.'

'Four in the morning!' Lorel made mock horror signs.

'It gets worse,' Chris informed her, grinning. 'Wait till the sun starts to climb . . . man, is it hot!'

Lorel eyed his tan. 'So I see. Don't you ever do any work?'

'Nope!' He jabbed the lift with a bony finger. 'I loaf about mainly, drinking and womanising.'

'Remind me to avoid you like the plague!' Lorel smiled.

'You're stuck with me, I'm afraid,' he drawled. 'I'm always on set.'

'Doing what?'

'Continuity,' he told her, and laughed. 'But I'm only an assistant, and very humble, once you get to know me. Steve says I'm a pain in the neck, but you won't listen to him, will you?'

Lorel's eyes shuttered and she said very coolly, 'Speaking of Mr Kennedy, why exactly couldn't he make it to the airport tonight?'

'I . . .' He looked away, flushing. 'A personal matter. I really can't discuss it. You know how it is . . .'

Yes, she knew exactly how it was. Her lips tightened and she got in the lift, riding up with the spindly Egyptian porter who carried her cases, keeping her face cool and remote until he had gone, then closing the door fast.

Damn him! Tears stung her eyes and she leant against the door, breathing erratically. He's made a fool of me again. Yet again! How many times did she have to learn what kind of man he was?

Her face burnt with anger and her heart was hurting badly. She went across to the windows and flung them open, glad of the rush of cool air on her cheeks. He wasn't going to ruin her first night in the land of the Pharoahs. She had wanted to see Egypt all her life, and now that she was here, she wasn't wasting it.

Lorel breathed in the city, smelt the potent mixture of poverty and wealth in the dirty, traffic-ridden streets. The noise was a culture shock in itself, and pure Cairo.

Looking down, she saw a taxi draw up and her body iced over as she saw the elegant blonde step out, Steve following her, bending his dark head to pay the driver.

Jealousy stabbed like a red-hot knife in her stomach as she watched Steve slide an arm around the blonde, who turned her head to look up into his eyes. Steve seemed to smile at her for a moment, then his head bent and their mouths met in a kiss.

Lorel stepped back as though slapped, staring at the shutters banging shut in a breeze from outside.

Steve Kennedy's kind of woman. Sophisticated, elegant and sure of herself. That blonde was no stranger to Lorel, she realised that now. She had seen her before, and the memory came spinning back to her.

It had been the night she drove down to Robert's. Steve had pulled up in his sleek Jaguar and the blonde had stepped out, wrapped in fur and diamonds with her husky voice and her long, cool smile.

Yes, she was Steve Kennedy's kind of woman, all right. Lorel fiercely swallowed her hurt pride and struggled to dismiss it from her mind, going into the shower and stripping quickly.

The jets of water almost punished her as she turned her face to them, standing weakly against the wall, her legs shaking as the shock of what she'd seen finally hit her and she began to cry.

It was a few minutes later that she heard the insistent knocking on the door, and she froze, her wet face icy with sudden nerves.

Twisting the shower off, she stepped out, wrapping a towel around herself.

'Who is it?'

There was a pause, then a heavily accented voice said in pidgin English, 'Room service. I have champagne—compliments Mr Kennedy.'

For a moment she felt nothing. The water dripped softly from her body to the floor, and she stared in silence at the door. Then her eyes closed at this, the final insult. All the anger dissolved on a sudden wave of pain and she faced the truth with dull acceptance. Steve did not love her. He never would. He was, as she had suspected, a womaniser. Oh, he was good. Practised, very convincing. He had made her believe he was to be trusted. He had made her believe he could fall in love with her. But tonight had ripped the veil from her eyes with brutal force, and she felt an emptiness seep through her heart that was a little like a stab wound.

Her hand shook as she opened the door and stepped back in silence. The slender Egyptian glanced at her from beneath heavy black lashes, then walked in, deposited the silver ice-bucket on her table, and left.

Lorel swallowed hard and went over to it, picking up the small card beside the spray of roses.

'Darling—forgive me. Something came up. Steve.'

Tears burnt her eyes and she trembled with a hatred that overwhelmed her. Had she not seen him in that bar? What if she had not glanced out of the window at the exact moment he was getting out of the taxi with the blonde? What then?

She would have believed him. Believed this hastily scrawled note and fallen for his clever strategy.

'Damn you!' Her fingers trembled as she ripped the note into tiny pieces and flung it in the waste-basket. Hatred burned in her heart and she clung to the edge of the table with white-knuckled hands, forcing herself to calm down inch by inch, until she was able to walk slowly across to her bed and begin unpacking, hanging her clothes in the neat, functional wardrobe.

The knock on the door sometime later did not surprise her. She knew who it was, and as she stared across at the door she felt an anger so forceful that she considered for a moment hurling the champagne bottle across the room and watching it shatter into a thousand pieces.

'Lorel?' Steve's deep, drawling voice made her stiffen. 'Are you there?'

Struggling for composure, she walked across to the door and pulled it open.

'What a day!' Steve just strode right past her and

into the room without a pause. 'I've been pulled every which way and turned inside-out. Thank God for you—you're the first piece of sanity to hit Cairo this week!'

Lorel stood by the open door, trembling with rage. The shock of seeing him had thrown her off balance, and her gaze ran quickly over his body, hungrily drinking in the taut, healthy muscles rippling at his arms, legs, shoulders. He wore faded jeans, tight on the long legs and slim hips. An open-necked white shirt showed the tanned column of his throat and network of black hairs on his chest.

'Ah!' He perched on the edge of the table, picking up the champagne. 'I could do with some of this! How was your flight?'

Lorel closed the door, tight-lipped. 'Fine.'

'Good,' he drawled, giving her a quick smile. 'Sorry I couldn't meet you. Something came up.'

Her smile was all ice. 'So you said in your note.' Inside, she was a mass of anger and resentment. What arrogance! How dared he walk in like this? And to take the champagne he had sent her! Had he just left the blonde with some excuse? Or was he planning to go back to her at any moment?

'Are you having some of this?' The long fingers ripped the gold from the neck of the bottle, and his thumbs pushed the cork upwards.

She watched him, her face cold and expressionless. An acute tension in the air reached him, and he stopped suddenly, looking up at her, his eyes narrowing on her icy face.

The champagne cork exploded with a loud bang.

A fierce white stream of champagne burst out of the neck and splattered his long hands, his jeans, the floor.

'Damn!' he muttered, quickly thrusting the bottle towards the two fluted glasses to catch the last of the overspill.

Lorel watched him, hating him. He sensed it, and put the champagne down with a cool thud, looking back at her in the tense silence.

'What's wrong?' he asked flatly.

Lorel kept her eyes expressionless. 'Nothing.'

'Come off it,' he said bluntly. 'You're all ice. What's happened—did Goodfellow say something to you at the airport?'

'What could he have said?' she asked quickly, watching his face.

He studied her through thick lashes. 'You tell me.'

Her mouth was a tight, angry line. 'He told me you'd been called away on an urgent matter.' Pausing, she added, 'A personal matter.'

Steve rapped long fingers on his denim-clad thigh. 'Yes?' he said, waiting. 'I don't see the problem.'

Lorel studied him for a moment with an anger that made her frightened. How could she feel this much towards one man?

Trembling, she decided to end this pointless, painful conversation.

'It's late. Would you mind if we continued this some other time?'

'Yes, I would mind,' he said grimly.

'I want to go to sleep.' Lorel coolly glanced at her watch. 'I have a make-up call at four.'

'Not until I find out what's bugging you.'

'I told you.' Her face and voice were indifferent. 'Nothing. I'm just tired.'

His eyes flashed. 'Don't lie to me.'

She looked him up and down with icy contempt. 'Why should I lie?'

He was silent for a moment, his jaw tight. 'I don't know, Lorel,' he said flatly. 'But I know you are.'

She smiled coldly. 'I see,' she said with utmost politeness.

He watched her broodingly as she walked to the bed and carefully closed her suitcase, her fingers trembling with the strain of keeping up this ice-cold front.

Steve said deeply, 'When I left England I thought we'd reached an agreement.'

'An agreement?' Her smile was all ice. 'I don't know what you're talking about.'

'All right—an understanding. Call it what you like. You seemed to have forgiven me.'

Lorel sat down on the bed and folded her hands on her lap, studying him with a polite smile. 'Go on.'

He drew a deep breath, the blue eyes flickering over her cold face. 'You said you were ready to forget what happened five years ago. Call it quits. Start getting to know me again.'

Lorel remembered the blonde by his side, the way he'd slid a casual arm around her shoulders and bent his dark head for a kiss. Anger and jealousy flared up inside her and turned her eyes a fierce bright green.

'Did I?' she said scornfully. 'I'd forgotten!'

His mouth tightened. He studied her for a moment

and the hostility crackled between them. Then he said under his breath, 'Why are you doing this?'

Her eyes flashed. 'Doing what?'

'You know damned well what!' He straightened, bristling with temper. 'If you felt this way, why didn't you say so at the time?'

'I was alone in that hotel room with you!' she said acidly. 'I would have been a fool to argue with you!'

His face hardened. 'You mean it was all lies? Every word?'

'That's right!' she said fiercely, glad to see she had hit him hard, a fierce pleasure racing across her heart as she saw the whiteness of his mouth and the way he held himself so stiffly. 'You were in an unbeatable position. You got me into that room against my will and then poured your story out in glorious Technicolour! What did you expect me to do? Slap your face?'

'I expected you to tell the truth!' he bit out.

'Liar! You expected me to fall into bed with you! You started to seduce me the minute we were inside the door!'

'I kissed you!' he said harshly. 'Nothing more!'

'That was enough!' She gave a bitter laugh, all the jealousy and pain of the last two hours blazing from her green eyes. 'And I just wanted to get away from you. So I said anything—anything you wanted to hear. And I didn't mean a word of it! Not one word!'

His face was a dark, angry red. 'You kissed me back!' he said through his teeth. 'You couldn't fake that much—not even if you were scared out of your wits!'

'I'm an actress—remember?' She laughed at him, glad she had hurt that all-powerful ego. 'Watch my love scenes with Prince Farouk when I make them! Maybe that'll convince you!'

There was a short, electric silence, and the emotion that flashed between them was white-hot, explosive, making them both tremble.

Then Steve moved. 'You damned little bitch!' he said hoarsely, and Lorel leaped up from the bed in alarm, trying to run past him, but he was too fast for her and his hands caught her wrists, dragging her towards him.

He caught her long hair in a cruel grip, ruthlessly ignoring her struggles, his face hard and violently angry as he bent his dark head to kiss her.

Lorel whimpered, her mouth crushed under the force of his, her hands trembling on his broad shoulders as he kissed her brutally, wanting to hurt her, and the long fingers of his other hand tightened mercilessly around her waist, holding her body so that she was crushed against him, a slender, struggling child-woman with no power at all.

Bitter tears stung her eyes and she tried to rip her mouth from his, but he held her fast, enjoying the pain he inflicted, his lips hard and punishing.

When at last he released her, tears were streaming over her cheeks and her mouth was bruised, swelling as she stared at him, breathing hard with an anger and hatred that frightened her.

The blue eyes flickered over her face, inspecting her with harsh satisfaction.

Lorel stared back at him, trembling. 'I hate you!'

she whispered fiercely. 'I'll never forgive you for this!'

'I don't want your forgiveness,' he said flatly. 'Keep it.'

Then he was gone, walking away from her and slamming the door behind him while she shook with a force of anger that was so foreign to her nature that it made her sink on to the bed as though her knees might give way at any moment. Her hands covered her face, while she cried bitterly, her shoulders shaking.

She had never in her life experienced such a tidal wave of emotion. Never spoken to anyone like that. Never felt that fierce need to hurt someone else so much that they could be pushed to the point of violence.

It shook her, and she fought for calm, going into the bathroom and splashing her face over and over with cold water until the thudding of her heart was stilled and the waves of anger dissipated, leaving her in a numb and inhuman state of exhaustion.

Crawling into bed, she flicked the light off and lay staring at the darkness in a dead silence, unable to sleep as the conversation was replayed over and over in her mind until she thought she might go mad.

She fell into a dreamless sleep and was woken at three a.m. by the telephone. Crawling out of bed, she felt as though she had been hit by a sledgehammer, and dressed in a vague, uncoordinated way before going downstairs to breakfast.

It was dark outside, and the breakfast-room was crowded with hungover crew and cast, eating with white, tired faces, dark circles under their eyes.

She saw Steve at once. His dark head was bent in conversation with the blonde-haired lady at his side, and as Lorel stared so he tensed, frowning, and turning to look across the crowded room with narrowed eyes.

Their eyes met. Lorel felt suddenly sick, and walked across to a table, sitting down shakily without looking back at Steve. She didn't want to know. She just didn't want to know.

They rode out to Gizeh for the filming at three-thirty in an air-conditioned coach. Lorel sat at the front, looking out into the night-darkened streets of Cairo and wondering if last night had really happened. The fierce, violent argument seemed almost dream-like. Yet the nagging ache in her heart was far too real for it to have been a dream.

Lorel waited patiently in her trailer while make-up and wardrobe worked on her. Outside, the Pyramids towered above the desert while dawn broke in streaks of red-gold light that fanfared a new day. A jackal howled against the dying of the light. Tourist police wandered around the film set in their black uniforms, inspecting the crew and cameras with interest.

Where was Steve? The desert wind ruffled her hair as she stared out of the window waiting to be called. Was he here with the rest of the crew, or was he elsewhere, with the beautiful blonde?

Lorel turned her attention to the script, trying to dismiss him from her mind. The script was based on the true story of Eleanor Browning, a young English girl who came to Egypt in 1890 with her father and was kidnapped by an Arab prince to be held as hostage against the authorities.

Prince Farouk snatched her on horseback while she was walking beside the Pyramids with her chaperon. He took her back to his encampment in the desert and held her there for two months.

But he fell in love with her, and eventually decided to release her back to her family. In the late nineteenth century, however, a young girl of noble birth was considered ruined if even seen out alone with a strange gentleman. For Eleanor to even attempt to re-enter polite society after being held hostage by an Arab prince in the desert was unthinkable, and a horrific scandal erupted around her. Labelled 'ruined' by her family and friends, Eleanor was immediately ineligible for marriage, and confined for the rest of her life to wear black and behave as a respectable matron.

Prince Farouk, on hearing of her fate, rode back to Cairo and snatched her again—this time for good.

He married her, made her a princess, and they lived in Arabia in a happy marriage for the next thirty years. Prince Farouk died in 1922, and Eleanor wrote her memoirs.

They were an immediately best-seller. The wheel of time had turned full circle, and Rudolf Valentino was the latest smash-hit as The Sheikh. The America of the 1920s welcomed Eleanor Browning with open arms.

At fifty-five, Eleanor moved to New York, living in a country estate in the Hudson Valley. Fêted and adored wherever she went, she made a fortune out of writing best-selling books based on her Arabian experiences.

She died aged seventy-one, a Grande Dame figure in New York, and never remarried. She was buried with photographs of her prince, still wearing the jewels he had given her.

'Miss Lane!'

Lorel jumped at the sound of her name, and went out of the trailer, to find that the sun was already burning demonically as she walked in the long, white lace dress to the cameras.

'When you see Prince Farouk,' Lunchino shielded his eyes against the glare of the sun, 'you do not at first realise he is after you. You merely look at his horse, then look away.'

'Do I keep on walking?' Lorel stood in front of the Great Pyramid, watching him, while the crew and extras stood around, half in period costume, half in jeans and T-shirts.

'Absolutely.' Luchino put her through her paces. 'Farouk will snatch you here.'

'In rehearsals at Elstree, I just let him pick me up. Is that what you want here?' Lorel asked.

'Let him do all the work!' Luchino laughed, eyes creasing. 'And struggle as much as you can. It must be realistic. Try to imagine exactly how terrified you would be if it happened to you.'

Lorel made a face. 'Pretty terrified!'

'Farouk will ride off into the desert with you—over the crest of that dune.' Luchino glanced at his watch. 'I don't want to film this more than once. Try to get it right on the first run. OK?'

Lorel nodded, and he moved away, clad in jeans

and a white bomber-jacket, looking far younger than his sixty-four years. Silver-haired and with keen blue eyes, he stayed youthful, with a zest for life and an energetic approach to everything he did.

'Action!'

'Scene Twelve, Take One,' droned a young man in T-shirt, clapperboard in front of the camera.

Lorel started walking, her heart thudding with nerves as she looked up at the tall yellow-stone Pyramid, the blue Egyptian sky fierce behind it as a breeze lifted white dust from the weather-beaten steps.

Hoof-beats thudded softly in the distance and Lorel turned, face coolly haughty as she glanced over one white shoulder.

Her companion was talking softly, saying irrelevant nothings under her breath. Lorel smiled at her and fanned herself as the period-dressed extras walked elegantly around the Pyramids.

Again Lorel turned. The Arab thundered down on her, handsome in white robes that flew out as he rode, flash of gold at his head-dress.

She frowned, staring in sudden alarm. There was something familiar about him . . . that tanned face and blue eyes . . . the way he rode with such masculine force.

Her eyes widened in sudden horror. It was Steve! The parasol dropped from her hand as she stared, her mouth falling open in shock as he thundered across the desert strip towards her.

'No!' Her scream pierced the morning air with a note of alarm that made even the extras catch their breath as Steve Kennedy bore down on her.

His arm lifted her and she struggled bitterly, punching and biting as he held her tightly, that strong arm implacable, and her dress tore along one thigh with a ferocious rip.

The stallion raced away past the startled extras, and Lorel continued her fierce struggles, her nails raking his face, making him swear as blood ran in thin strips along his cheekbone. His arm tightened, hurting her until she could scarcely breath, holding her clamped against his body, her face bumping hard against his.

They galloped over the tallest sand-dune and she stared over his powerful shoulders at the Sphinx and Pyramids so far below.

'Steve!' Breathless, she screamed at him above the rushing wind and thundering hooves, her nostrils filled with the scent of his sweat, his skin, the hot, wet skin of the horse.

But he carried her remorselessly into the desert, holding her hand against his body as her breasts hit his hard chest, hurting her until she gasped against his dark throat, burying her face in terror in case she fell off this nightmarishly fast stallion.

CHAPTER EIGHT

RACING across endless desert sands, Lorel clung to Steve, beginning to feel real anxiety about her situation now that they were alone in this vast emptiness with nothing but sand and infinite sky around them. Had he gone mad? Why didn't he stop? Her heart lurched as she considered her chances of survival if he was planning to rape her. Realistic appraisal put them at virtually nil. And she saw no other reason for this frightening ride into nothingness.

She didn't even know enough about him to be sure of her safety. The realisation was like a hammer-blow to her consciousness, and she suddenly went ice-cold with fear. What could she do? How could she defend herself? The world kaleidoscoped into something approaching another dimension as she realised how much in very real danger she could well be.

Then it was over. The horse pulled up with a fierce cry as Steve reined the animal in, its nostrils flaring and sweat gleaming on its rich, white coat.

Steve looked down at her, the blue eyes framed by the white of his head-dress, one side draped right across his face to hide his identity. Lorel did not speak or breath, a wave of *déjà vu* holding her frozen for a moment as she looked at those winged black brows, piercing blue eyes, all framed by the cool,

141

white linen.

The horse danced elegantly beneath them. Steve's arm tightened on her. The stallion swished its white tail and snorted in the silence.

'Get down,' Steve said harshly.

Lorel slithered off the saddle, her legs trembling as she landed in the hot yellow sands.

'Does Luchino know it was you?' she asked huskily.

He swung off the horse with masculine grace. 'It was his idea. We needed that scene completed before the tourists arrived. You had to get it right first time, and for that—you needed to look really scared.'

A smile pulled her lips and she said huskily, 'You certainly got your wish!'

'Yes,' he said flatly. 'And I'm not sure how I feel about that.'

Her eyes shot to his. 'It was a shock, that's all. I'd expected to see Johnny Valentine.'

'You won't see him till at least midday,' Steve drawled coolly. 'He's being sobered up back at the hotel. Too much whisky last night.'

She laughed shakily and shook her head, nervous under that watchful gaze. 'It's true what they say about him, then? I always thought it was publicity.' Johnny Valentine, with his deep, rich voice and unstable black eyes, danced on a knife-edge of destruction, yet his electrifying performances kept him at the top of his profession, and Lorel admired him enormously.

'He's a bloody liability,' Steve said caustically. 'And he's getting worse. I think he's actually on the verge of serious alcoholism, and that's not funny. Or glamorous.'

Lorel looked at him, a shadow crossing her eyes. 'We all have an Achilles heel,' she said softly, 'don't we?'

There was an odd silence, and she felt her mouth go dry as she heard the soft moan of the desert breeze on sand and sky, saw it ripple Steve's white bedouin robes and black hair.

'What would you know about it?' Steve's voice was oddly hoarse. 'You've never really cared for anyone. Never had a fatal weakness. An Achilles heel.'

Lorel moistened her lips, looking away. 'Shouldn't we be getting back? They might be worried.'

His mouth tightened. 'I'm not ready to take you back yet.'

'But the filming . . .' she began huskily, and his eyes flashed.

'To hell with it!' he said under his breath. 'I haven't been able to think about the film for weeks!'

Her eyed widened at that, but she struggled to remain composed. 'I've thought of nothing else!' she lied.

'And I was too blind to see it,' he said tightly, coming towards her. 'You used me, didn't you? To get what you wanted. What's the old cliché? Treat them mean, keep them keen . . . I've used it often enough myself. God knows, I never thought it would rebound on me like this.'

The sheer satisfaction of knowing she had hurt his ego showed in her eyes in a brief flash of triumph, and that was a mistake, because she saw an answering light of hard, cold anger in his.

'It's true, then,' he said roughly, mouth tight. 'You strung me along. The whole thing, from start to finish. Tell me—did you plan it, or did it just snowball?'

'I . . .' Her breath hurt as she stared at him, pleasure mingling with pain. 'I don't remember.'

'Sure you do,' he drawled tightly. 'Clever little strategists like you never forget their game-plans! What interests me is whether or not you recognised me. It certainly hooked my interest—it made me want you. Was that part of it?'

'Why does that matter now?' she stammered.

'It hurt my ego, darling,' he said under his breath. 'And that's the most vulnerable place to aim.'

Pain turned her face to a white mask and she said bitterly, 'It shouldn't be! If you were any kind of a man, it would be your heart!'

His eyes flashed. 'You want that too, do you?' His mouth tightened. 'You greedy little bitch! You can think again. Whatever else you've taken from me, you'll never get that. I wouldn't hand it over to a cheap little tramp like you!'

She flinched. 'Cheap?' Her head lifted stiffly. 'I don't think so! From what you've said, it cost you a lot to try and get me.'

He looked murderous for a moment, and alarm made her body tense for flight, seeing the red stain of rage run over his cheekbones, his nostrils flaring as he stood watching her in disbelief.

'You're no different from the rest,' he said roughly, struggling to keep his temper in check. 'All you want is your name in lights. And you're prepared to play casting-couch tease until you get it, aren't you?'

Tears stung the back of her eyes. 'Why not? It's a tough business. The toughest. No one else will watch out for me. If I played dirty, it was because men like you forced me into it.' The lies fell out so easily, tumbling from her mouth instead of the awful pain that clawed at her as she realised just how little he really cared for her. She had been just another conquest, another actress to pass the time with.

'Sure,' Steve drawled unpleasantly, 'and if you say that often enough to yourself, you might be able to look in the mirror again one day.'

Hot colour flooded her face. 'I can live with myself!'

'Can you?' he said hoarsely. 'I can't! I don't like being played for a fool, Lorel. It makes me angry. It makes me want to hit back.'

Her heart missed a beat at the look in his eyes and she found herself taking a nervous step back from him, her legs suddenly weak with alarm.

'You're right to be scared,' he said under his breath, and the cool eyes flicked from side to side slowly, then back at her. 'We're quite alone out here.'

As if in reply, the desert breeze rushed warm fingers over her face, lifting her hair in damp strands from her face as she stared at him, her heart thudding a frightened beat.

He moved forwards, eyes intent. 'You thought I was powerless once you got to Cairo, didn't you?

Thought I'd be too humiliated to do anything about it.'

Her mouth went dry. 'I . . .'

'Well, you really picked the wrong man to play with. I don't like cheats. Particularly when they turn as vicious as you did last night!'

She was backing away fast, her eyes wide. 'I had to say something!'

'You said quite enough!' he bit out. 'Now it's my turn. Only I'm not going to bother with words to show you what I think of you!'

His hands shot out, caught her shoulders and dragged her towards him, but she struggled fiercely, kicking his shins and raking his hands with her nails. He muttered something vicious under his breath and Lorel escaped.

Then she was running, her heart pounding like a sledgehammer as she felt the sweat run down between her breasts, over her thighs and stomach, the heavy dress cumbersome. Breathing in rough gasps, she turned and saw him hot on her heels, his face white with fury. She put on speed, desperately, but her foot caught in the hem of her dress and she cried out, falling clumsily face down in the sand.

His shadow fell over her, she gasped for breath and turned, lying on her back to stare up at him.

'Stay like that!' he said hoarsely, and dropped to his knees. 'I like to see you helpless!'

'Don't!' she cried out in breathless panic, but he was already pushing her back against the sand, his mouth covering hers in a burning, punishing kiss, making her moan as his lips crushed hers, hurting her deliberately and leaving her in no doubt about his feelings towards her as he used her brutally.

'Lie still!' he muttered thickly as she struggled.

Tears burned over her lashes, spilling on to her cheeks with a fierce mingling of pleasure and pain as she kissed him back with everything she had, her body sliding against his in torment and bitter hatred of her need for him.

Suddenly, he raised his head, breathing in rough gasps, his eyes almost dazed as he stared down at her, one hand sliding from her breast down to her naked waist, the fingers hard and punitive.

'I really showed you what I thought of you, didn't I?' he said bitterly, and his mouth shook as he looked back at her. 'You must be laughing yourself sick over me!'

He rolled away suddenly, sitting up, one knee bent as he rested his arm on it, fingers drumming restlessly on his mouth as he stared into the desert without another word.

Lorel stared at him, frozen where she lay and studying that hard profile, seeing the bitter lines of rage and resentment at his hard mouth.

He looked across at her. 'Get dressed!' His voice was a hoarse whisper filled with disgust, and she whitened, stung into movement by it; sitting up and dragging her dress back up over her bare torso while he watched, making her fumble, her cheeks flushing scarlet as she saw the sheer contempt in his eyes.

When she had finished, he got to his feet. 'We'd better get back,' he said tightly. 'They'll be worried.'

Stumbling under that scathing glance, Lorel fol-

lowed him to the horse. It danced elegantly and
bowed its white head; Steve patted its slender neck,
whispering gentle words of endearment to it, and she
felt an ache that was unbearable in her heart as she
realised he had never spoken to her with the
tenderness he had just shown this horse.

He mounted gracefully, reins gathered in one
hand, and looked down at her. Lorel could not meet
his eyes, filled with a self-hatred that made her want
to cry.

He reached down and lifted her roughly, and she
sat astride the horse in front of him, one bare thigh
glistening beneath the sun. Steve kicked the horse
into action, and a moment later they were galloping
across the desert, the wind rushing through their hair
and the horse's hooves thundering, kicking up yellow
dust, sweat breaking out on its shoulders as Lorel
clung to Steve's hands and the saddle.

They were over the tall dune before she had caught
her breath, thundering down into the valley where
the Pyramids stood timelessly, surrounded by cast
and crew and a handful of early tourists.

They all looked at her with knowing eyes as she
rode back to the set with Steve, and her face flushed
dark red as she realised that what they thought had
happened was exactly what *had* happened.

Steve deposited her on the flat sandstone, surveying her bruised mouth and tear-stained face. 'You've
been crying,' he said slowly, and one finger traced
her tears. 'I'm sorry.'

White-faced, she jerked back from his touch.
'Forget it.'

His hand dropped to his side, his mouth tightening. 'It won't happen again. I can assure of that. From now on, I'll steer clear of you.'

Her mouth trembled and she looked away. A flash of bright yellow hair caught her eye, and her heart twisted with fierce jealousy as she saw the blonde woman stepping elegantly from an open-topped jeep, swaying towards them in dark blue silk.

Jealousy stung her. 'I'm sure you won't lack for female company!'

'So am I!' he said tightly. 'The sooner I forget you, the better.'

She looked at him, eyes fierce. 'I thought you already had. Every time I see you you're with her! Here she comes now. Don't let me get in your way!'

He frowned, studying her. 'What the hell are you talking——'

'Darling! Where have you been?' The husky French voice startled them both, and the horse danced as Steve straightened, turning to watch the blonde approach, her hips swaying, shielding her eyes with a shiny clutch bag.

'You're up early, Katya,' Steve straightened. 'I thought we were having lunch, not breakfast.'

'I couldn't sleep,' she said huskily, and there were shadows under her eyes.

His eyes narrowed. 'Trouble?' he said quickly, deeply.

'No more than usual . . .' Her voice trailed off and she looked away, her white skin almost bruised beneath those crystalline eyes. 'It's such a pretty morning!' Turning her face up to Steve's, she smiled, her hand sliding over his tightly. 'Let's spend it together, darling.'

'Sure.' His face softened and he drawled, 'There's no one else I'd rather be with.'

It was a deliberate slap in the face to Lorel and she knew it, her face tightening with intolerable jealousy and humiliation.

Steve looked down at her, his eyes cold. 'I'll go and change. Hadn't you better go back to make-up, Lorel?'

She nodded stiffly, turning on her heel. Steve was walking the horse over to a separate trailer. Lorel had gone but a few yards when Katya's voice stopped her. 'You're Lorel?'

It froze her in her tracks and she turned, her face tight, looking back. They studied each other, ice in their eyes. Lorel felt trapped in an appalling farce, staring at Katya and seeing the perfection of her beauty, knowing she could never compete with that classical face and mannequin-slim body. In her dusty, tattered dress, hair escaping in bright red tendrils around a sweaty, tear-stained face, she felt awkward and unattractive. Katya was her complete opposite; she suggested air and water, Lorel suggested fire and earth.

The hostility in Katya's eyes was unmistakable. 'You are not what I expected,' she said with Parisian scorn.

'Oh?' Lorel said tightly, her eyes reflecting every bit as much hatred. 'I wasn't aware I'd been talked about.'

Katya laughed. 'You held up filming for three

weeks. Did you think no one would notice?'

'I didn't intend to do that,' Lorel said angrily. 'It wasn't planned.'

'No?' Katya's lashes flicked, sending her icy gaze skimming over Lorel's sensually dishevelled appearance and making her burn with rage at the contempt in the other woman's eyes.

'No!' Lorel turned on her heel before she lost her temper and walked back across the sun-bleached land, her heart pounding with unleashed temper and indignation at the obvious message in Katya's eyes. She thought Lorel had deliberately thrown a spanner in the works to get attention! How dared she?

Or did she? In the stifling heat of the trailer, Lorel paused, her eyes narrowing. Maybe Katya knew about her involvement with Steve, too. Yes. That must be it. It had not been professional contempt she had seen in Katya's face, but jealousy.

Her hands clenched. What a web of deceit! Steve was playing them off against each other. Her eyes closed and she leaned weakly against the trailer door, swatting a fly that landed on her arm and then buzzed away. How did I ever fall in love with a man capable of this? she thought. He was hurting everyone around him. Using them, lying to them. And quite blatantly. Did he think they were both stupid, she and Katya? Did he honestly think they would stand it much longer?

She had seen the look on Katya's face: hostility and dislike blazing out of those ice-cold eyes. And Lorel knew only too well what her own face must have reflected—all the jealousy and torment of the last twenty-four hours.

Glancing bitterly out of the trailer door, she saw Steve walk arrogantly over to Katya, his clothes coolly Western now, the white jeans and short-sleeved white shirt showing the long, masculine lines of his body. Katya was smiling at him, her eyes bright.

Lorel felt sick to her stomach, watching Steve slide an arm around Katya, pull her close to him and kiss her mouth just before they walked to the jeep together and drove away.

She stared after them until the dust from the jeep wheels was a dim yellow cloud on the horizon. Then the tears burned her eyes and she walked unsteadily to the dressing-table, sitting down and staring in the mirror at her dirty, dishevelled appearance.

Hot colour flooded her face. Was this what she really looked like? Turning her face this way and that, she felt bitterness touch her mouth. No wonder Katya had looked at her with such scorn. She looked like a raggle-taggle gypsy!

As for Steve—the though of his touching her again made her stomach knot with distaste. He was a liar and a cheat, and she was well rid of him.

Pain flooded through her and her mouth trembled. She felt weak and helpless and stupid and humiliated.

How did it happen? How did I fall in love with him? she thought wearily. Her eyes closed and she bent her head. There was no one moment, no point at which she could say for certain that it had happened. And no way out of this terrible, aching sense of emptiness and loss.

He had broken through her barriers, forced her into a passionate response she had thought she was incapable of. Now she was left with nothing but self-disgust for ever allowing him to kiss her.

The scene in the desert replayed in her mind with burning intensity. She felt his hands on her breasts, the salt-sweet touch of his mouth on hers, the tangle of their bodies and the hoarse moan of his mouth on her throat as he slid his hands over her naked waist.

Her eyes flared open. Was that really her? Her heart thundered into life as she stared at her reflection, seeing not the dishevelled creature unworthy of respect or attention from a cool Parisian lady.

The woman who stared back at her was a red-haired creature of impossible sexuality, shoulders bare and smudged with dirt, sweat-stained face, and red, bruised lips that pouted and shrieked touch-ability. And her eyes. They were the most revealing. She could send herself mad staring into them and wondering if they belonged to her, for they burned with a fierce green intensity that was almost breath-taking, raging with emotions, cross-currents of jeal-ousy and hate, need and desire, rage and forgiveness.

He's made me feel it all, she thought incredu-lously, staring. He woke me up and broke me down and brought me alive until I'm so caught up in him and what I feel for him that I've become some other woman, not the Lorel I was before he arrived.

Looking back on her life before he arrived was like looking back at a frightened child-woman stumbling through a desert, afraid to look to left or right, afraid to feel or reach out for human contact. Particularly from men. Exclusively from men.

Her crush on Robert had been childish. Like a teenager kissing a poster of David Bowie before she went to sleep. Hugging a record of David Cassidy close to her heart and singing, 'How Can I Be Sure?' along with his soft adolescent voice.

Steve Kennedy had changed all that. His sheer masculinity and sophistication had broken down the frontiers of adolescence before she was ready to cope with the feelings she would find on the other side of that high fence.

So she had run. Turned tail and scampered back into safety like a little fieldmouse. And she had lain dormant ever since.

Now he was back, and with every moment that she looked at him, every moment that she thought of him, his hold on her became stronger.

Slowly, she lifted her trembling hand to her mouth and traced the bruised outline, longing to find some trace of his kiss. Her heart thudded faster and she felt her mouth go dry. Excitement and self-awareness were growing. She could scarcely hold the thoughts that tumbled into her mind.

I do like it. I do enjoy his touch. I do want him. Oh, God, I do! Her eyes closed and she drew a shaky breath, recognising her sexuality as it suddenly blazed through her in waves of delicious freedom.

Then it stopped. Frozen and in limbo. 'But he doesn't want me!' she whispered, and tears slipped silently over her lashes.

She smiled thinly, hands toying with the row of brushes on the dressing-table. Her make-up artist had neatly stacked various pots and creams beside the mirror, ready to make her look suitably ravished later on.

This is my world. And it isn't real. It revolves around make-believe. I go in front of cameras and pretend to be someone else. I wear strange clothes and speak in different accents and say words other people have written for me.

And there was nothing else in her life but acting. There never had been, not since she had made that overnight decision five years ago to become an actress. Straight after her night of confusion with Steve Kennedy.

Now, he was the only real thing in her life. The only part of her life that made her blood throb with adrenalin, made her glad that she was alive.

He was the wind in her hair, the touch of silk on her skin, the powerful roar of an engine as he drove her across a country that was his. Steve lived in the real world, and Lorel hungered to be with him in it. But he didn't want her there. He had made that only too plain.

She buried her face in her hands, whispering his name. He probably felt something for her, or he wouldn't have been so emotional in the desert. That rage in his eyes had not sprung from indifference. But he didn't feel enough. Not enough for Lorel—and certainly not enough for both of them.

She needed security as much as she needed the passion he fired in her. Steve was only prepared to offer fierce lovemaking and a love affair that would eventually destroy her.

No, she could not accept that from him. She needed more than that. And, however badly she hurt now, she would eventually get over it.

Determinedly, she went out into the hot sun and watched the technicians loading the equipment into the cars, ready to set up the next scene further up in the desert.

One or two of them stared at her, lazy grins on their sweaty faces as they raked their gazes over her. Lorel felt her hips sway, her body move with sensual grace.

This was what they wanted. This red-haired creature blazing with sexuality. And this was what Steve wanted. He wanted exactly what she had shown him the night she'd tried to seduce him in the hotel in Leysham. She hadn't even known it was in her. Hadn't been aware she was capable of it.

Johnny Valentine was lying flat in the sand with a panama hat over his eyes and a cigarette dangling from his lips.

Lorel took a deep breath and went over to introduce herself. At least it would take her mind off Steve, and she needed that desperately.

'Mr Valentine?'

Slowly, he pushed his hat back with one finger. Bloodshot eyes surveyed her and his head swayed as he lifted it inch by inch.

'Thank God!' he drawled in Shakespearean tones. 'Someone who looks worse than I do.'

She made a face. 'Thanks!'

He studied her unsteadily, then slapped the sand beside him. 'Sit down. Tell me all about it. Was it gin or a man?'

'The latter.' Lorel sat down cross-legged and sighed.

Johnny studied her lazily. 'At least he can't damage your liver. And for that, you should be thankful.'

She laughed. 'An interesting point!'

'Only time will mend your broken heart,' drawled Johnny. 'Just as only time will mend his broken legs!'

Lorel gave him an amused look. 'That was Miss Piggy,' she pointed out.

'I'm an actor,' drawled Johnny, going back under his hat. 'I just read the lines. Besides—I've always had a soft spot for Miss Piggy. She's a hard-headed pig. And I need someone tough to keep me out of trouble.' He looked at her sideways, his mouth curving like a dissolute earl's. 'Are you strong enough for the job?'

'I doubt it!' she laughed.

'No, you need protecting yourself, don't you?' He drew on his cigarette, then flicked it between long fingers in a glittering arc across the desert.

She studied him, frowning. 'Do I?'

'Stands out a mile, darling.' He slid his hat back over his face. 'You're even more hopeless than I am. An unstable bunch, us actors. We need big, strong guardian angels.' He laughed. 'Let's hope we find them.'

Lorel sighed. Perhaps he was right.

'Damned flies,' Johnny muttered, swatting one. 'I feel like a piece of ham on a hot day in Neasden.' He laughed. 'God! Wouldn't the critics have a field day if they heard me say that!'

'They do rather go for your throat, don't they?'

'Can't think why!' he drawled with a lazy smile. 'But God help me if I can't remember a damned thing about this film. What's the plot-line?'

Lorel laughed and outlined it for him, finding his copy of the script tucked into his jacket pocket with a woman's telephone number scrawled across it, frayed and battered and covered in coffee stains.

They read over it until Luchino called them, and the day passed with more hard work than Lorel had ever done in her life before. Filming went on until the last rays of light had disappeared, and she was exhausted. There had been torrid scenes, and endless waiting around between shots. She felt dirty and dusty and ready to collapse.

By the time she got back to the hotel, she was aching with tiredness. Quickly, she took a shower, washed the grime and sweat out of her hair, and then slipped into her oyster-pink silk nightgown, collapsing on the bed and falling asleep almost immediately.

CHAPTER NINE

THE voices woke her, filtering through her unconscious and forcing her awake. For a moment, Lorel just lay still, staring into the darkness of her bedroom. The oyster-pink nightgown was tangled at her thighs, she felt sluggish, still half asleep. Then she heard them again, soft and insistent, floating through the open shuttered doors leading to her balcony. A man's voice, deeply familiar, made her frown, and she got out of bed and walked barefoot to the shutters, stepping out on to the balcony without thinking.

She leapt back as if burnt, her heart thumping. Steve and Katya stood on the cold stone balcony next to hers, soft light from the bedroom flooding out on to their shadowed faces.

They wore matching bathrobes, their hair still wet from a shower, their legs and feet bare. Obviously nude beneath the white robes, their bodies were relaxed and easy with each other. Like lovers.

Lovers! Oh, God, she wasn't prepared for this. Sick waves of jealousy flooded over her and she leant weakly against the doorway of her bedroom, hidden in the shadows.

'It hurt him terribly to think it was you,' Katya was saying huskily. 'You were always his favourite . . .'

'It works both ways.' Steve's voice was deep, angry. 'I look on him as a father. I always have. You know that—why doesn't he?'

'Forgive him, Steve. He's insane with jealousy. Every time he looks at you he's not seeing you as you really are. He only sees you making love to me. What do you think that does to him?'

Steve drew a rough breath. 'I know, I know . . .' He looked away, his mouth tight as he studied the glittering Cairo horizon. 'Do you think he'll go through with it?'

'He's threatened divorce so many times before.' Katya shrugged elegant shoulders. 'Who knows? Maybe. Yes. it's just possible that this time he will go through with it.'

Lorel closed her eyes weakly. Adultery . . . she hadn't realised he was this despicable.

'What will you do?' Steve asked deeply.

'God knows. Try to talk him out of it.'

'I'll speak to him.'

She laughed. 'He won't listen to you!'

'I'll make him listen!'

'No, Steve.' Her voice was soft, firm, lightly accented. 'He's unreasonable at the moment. There's no point.'

'There's every point,' said Steve flatly. 'I'll tell him we're just good friends. That there's nothing between us. That——'

'Oh, Steven!' Katya whispered fiercely. 'Do you honestly think he'll believe that?'

His mouth was an angry line. 'I can't just sit back and——'

He broke off as there was a loud knock at his door that sent both him and Katya into sudden frozen silence, their heads turning to stare in through the open shutter windows. Lorel could almost hear their hearts beating with sudden shock as they stood closer together, their faces lined with tension and guilt.

'It's him!' Katya said shakily. 'I know it is.'

Steve drew a rough breath, looking at her. 'He'll kill us both if he finds you here like that.' The blue eyes raked her from her damp head to her bare legs.

'Where can I hide?' Katya's eyes darted wildly, and her hand trembled as she held Steve's arm for support.

'Nowhere,' he said flatly. 'He'll search the room.'

'Oh, God!' Katya buried her white face in her hands, trembling.

'Pull yourself together!' Steve said grimly, taking her shoulders and slipping a hand beneath her chin to force her head up. 'You've got to save your marriage, and you won't do that by hiding in my wardrobe. Think, Katya! Stay calm.'

'I can't . . .' Katya whispered, tears slipping out from her eyes. 'I can't face him. Not like this.'

'You have to,' Steve said firmly. 'Anything else will be an admission of guilt.'

'And what is this?' She looked down at herself, then at him, and her slender hand reached out to touch his tanned chest as she said huskily, 'We look such obvious lovers, my darling.'

Steve's mouth hardened. 'Let him think what he likes. I've had enough of his temper. It's time he faced the truth.'

'Open this door, Kennedy!' said an icy voice outside, and Lorel stood poised for flight, not wanting to be a witness to what was about to happen, hating herself for being so weak as to listen in the first place.

Steve turned and walked into the bedroom, leaving Katya standing motionless on the balcony, staring in, the light falling in cool white shafts on her shadowed face.

Lorel did not dare move or breathe. At one point, Katya actually looked straight at her, and Lorel held her breath, sure she had been seen. Then she looked away again, and Lorel's breath escaped in an inaudible sigh.

The door was pulled open. There was a silence.

'Come in, Max.'

The door closed firmly. A silence, then footsteps moving towards the open shutters and a silver-haired man stepped on to the balcony and into Lorel's eye-line, making her jaw drop with instant recognition.

Max Balanchine stood with icy dignity, his face tight with rage as he flicked silver-grey eyes over his wife, contempt making her tremble visibly.

'Did you have to make it so cheap?' he said icily.

Katya flinched. 'It's not what it seems . . .'

'Shut up!' His mouth hardened. 'Don't compound your guilt by lying.'

'She's not,' Steve said deeply, stepping forwards on the balcony, hands deep in his robe pockets. 'We're not lovers, Max. There's nothing between——'

'Then why are my wife's clothes on your bed?' Max asked politely. 'Why have you both so obviously just showered?'

'Look at her clothes, Max,' Steve said flatly. 'Look at mine. They're covered in mud. We had an accident in the jeep. Ran into some kind of bog just outside Saqqara——'

'And what were you doing in Saqqara?' Max asked icily. 'Why were you out with my wife——'

'For God's sake!' Steve said harshly. 'I've known her for years! Why shouldn't I take her out occasionally? We practically grew up in the film industry together. We shared a flat in Paris—long before she even met you, Max. She's one of my oldest friends.'

There was a flash of silver rage in the older man's eyes. 'Does that give you the right to continue your affair throughout my marriage?'

Steve looked at him angrily, his mouth hard. 'Katya was right. There's no point in talking to you!'

'Perhaps not,' Max said icily. 'I'll leave it all to my lawyers.'

There was a deathly hush. Katya was pale, staring at her husband. He held himself erect, dreessed exquisitely in black, and Lorel's heart went out to him. A man of such great dignity being humiliated like this. She could scarcely believe Steve was capable of it. Or Katya. Max Balanchine was a legend in European films. Publicity-shy, he kept his distance from the gutter press, rarely appearing in public, except at the opening nights of his films. He was a producer whose name was spoken in hushed tones of respect by all who worked with him or knew him.

'Max . . .' Katya said huskily, staring. 'You can't

mean to do this . . .'

'I'm afraid I already have, my dear.' He studied her coldly. 'I contacted my lawyers in Switzerland this afternoon.'

Steve drew a ragged breath, raking a hand through his hair. 'I don't believe this is happening! It's so——'

'Stupid?' Max raised silver brows. 'Pointless? I agree. But I have no time to waste on fighting my wife's lover to keep her affections.'

'Oh, I see!' Steve nodded, his mouth curling in an angry sneer. 'We're getting to the bottom line, now, are we? Time? The fact that you're pushing sixty and your lovely wife is twenty years younger? You can't stand that, can you, Max? It doesn't strike you as fair. You keep thinking she might prefer someone a little more energetic, a little——'

'Shut up!' Max said fiercely, shaking.

'Younger, shall we say?' Steve went on brutally. 'Someone who can better satisfy her——'

'Steve, for God's sake!' Katya clutched his arm but he shook her off.

'No, Katya! It has to be said!' He looked back at Max angrily. 'He has to face the truth before he destroys us all!'

'And have you faced the truth?' Max said hoarsely. 'Has Katya? Does she know about your little red-headed mistress?'

Steve went deathly still. 'I don't know what you're talking about!'

'Yes, you do, Steve,' Max said in a silvery voice, his eyes flashing with a glimmer of vengeance. 'The woman you made love to in the desert toay. Oh, yes—I heard about that. I heard how she stormed off when my wife came on the scene, too. What was wrong? Didn't she like your brand of lovemaking?'

Steve was white, his mouth shaking. 'You bastard!'

'Losing your touch, Steve?'

'Shut up!'

Max laughed. 'Not quite so keen on the truth now, are you, Steve? Not when it's aimed at you!'

'What do you know about the truth?' Steve said hoarsely, his eyes fierce. 'I was in love with her!'

Lorel gave a sharp cry of anguish and stumbled back into her bedroom, breathing harshly, uncaring that she had been both seen and heard, that they now knew she'd been listening as her shadowy figure turned sharply, the flash of oyster-pink silk as she turned like a banner in the night, as all three of them turned to stare at her with startled eyes.

'Oh, God . . . !' Steve said thickly. 'She must have heard every damned word!'

'Now see what you've done!' Katya flared angrily at her husband. 'You selfish man! You don't care who you hurt, who you humiliate!'

'Tht's not true!' Max said hoarsely. 'I—'

Lorel put her hands over her ears, lying face-down on the bed, tears burning over her lashes. She didn't give a damn any more what was said, who loved whom, or whether he was having an affair with another man's wife. She just didn't care.

He had used her. He was still using her. Using her to cover his affair with Katya Balanchine. Sick

jealousy made her fists clench as she buried her face
in the pillow, breathing in rough gasps.

Oh, God, why had she listened? She had had so
many chances to turn and leave. Yes, they might have
seen her. But what did it matter? At least she
wouldn't have heard what was being said, at least she
wouldn't have to carry their angry, vicious words
around in her head for the rest of her life. At least she
wouldn't have known exactly what kind of man
Steve Kennedy was.

She had told herself at the time that she couldn't
leave because they might have seen her. But that was
just lying to herself. That was an excuse she had
made to herself in order to stay. To eavesdrop.

It hurt her even more to know she was capable of
it. Like opening someone else's letters or reading
someone else's diary. It was the kind of thing she had
never thought she would do. Eavesdrop like Keyhole
Kate with her long, thin nose and great big ears.

The knock at the door made her gasp, her head
jerking up.

'Open it, Lorel!'

Steve's dark, angry voice made her tense, feeling
small and vulnerable and ashamed.

He rattled the door-handle. 'You have no choice,
Lorel. Open it!

Her lids closed and she realised he was right. Not
only did all three of them know for sure that she was
there and she had been listening, but Max Balanchine
was not a man who would take this sort of thing
lightly. He could fire her if she tried to get away with
this. Perhaps he already did intend to fire her. Per-

haps that was why Steve had come to her door.

Weakly, she got off the bed and shrugged into her matching wrap, opening the door.

His mouth was tight as he flicked contemptuous eyes over her. 'Eavesdropping,' he said flatly. 'I never thought you'd stoop so low.'

He came in, slamming the door behind him, and Lorel backed instinctively.

'What about you?' she said huskily. 'You're no better! That's how we met—remember? You eavesdropped on me and Robert in the garden!'

He stopped, eyes angry. 'That was different.'

'How was it?'

'Because I couldn't have moved away without being seen!'

'Neither could I!'

He laughed. 'Don't lie to yourself! You wouldn't have been noticed if you'd been clever about it.'

Hot colour flooded her face and she turned away, saying fiercely, 'All right! I coud have moved away. But I . . .' Her face burned and she said in a low voice, 'I didn't want to. I couldn't help myself. I had to listen.'

He was silent for a moment, then said deeply, 'How much did you hear?'

She shrugged, running a hand through her hair. 'Quite a lot. I don't know . . . I was listening before Max came in, if that's what you mean.'

He was silent again and she heard him breathing.

Lorel swallowed, unnerved, needing to talk, needing to fill the silence, terribly aware of his tall, lean body standing so close behind her in the dark room.

'I was asleep,' she said huskily. 'Your voices woke me. I went out on to the balcony without thinking. By the the time I realised what was being said . . .' Her voice trailed off and she bit her lip, lowering her head. How damning it sounded. Even to her.

'Enjoy yourself?' he said bitingly.

She flushed hotly and turned to look at him. 'I'm sorry!'

His mouth tightened and he thrust his hands deep in the pockets of the white robe, studying her. 'What do you intend to do?'

She stared, uncomprehending.

'With the story,' he said flatly. 'With what you know.'

Lorel was frowning. 'I don't understand . . .'

'Sure you do!' he drawled tightly. 'Shrewd little gold-digger like you. You could make a lot of money out of this. Either Max will pay you to keep your mouth shut, or the Press will pay you to open it up wide.' His dark eyes flicked over her with contempt. 'Which is it to be?'

Stung, she said fiercely, 'I don't want your money!'

'Ah.' He nodded, his mouth hard. 'A part in another picture. Of course. I should have guessed.'

'No!'

'How stupid of me!' he said tightly. 'It was what you wanted from me. What you got, too. You're one jump ahead of us all the time, aren't you?'

'I didn't even remember you!' Lorel cried. 'How could I have been——'

'Didn't you?' He stepped closer, his eyes fierce. 'I wonder! If it was a ruse to get me hooked, it certainly worked like a charm! You ran, and I chased!'

'It wasn't,' she said angrily, her face white. 'It was genuine!'

He gave a harsh crack of laughter. 'Don't try and keep it up, darling! I know exactly what you are now, and I ain't buying it!'

Lorel stared at him with absolute hatred, her mouth white and shaking with rage. 'How dare you talk to me like that?' she said unsteadily. 'How dare you?'

He studied her for a long moment, then drawled, 'You're good, I'll give you that. I almost believe you think you have a right to be offended!'

'I have every right!' she said hoarsely. 'You hypocritical bastard! How dare you come in here and preach morals to me? You're having an affair with another man's wife. Breaking up a marriage!'

'Oh, come off it!' he bit out. 'You know damned well I'm not!'

'Oh, I imagined it all, did I?' she said under her breath, pointing at the balcony. 'I imagined Max coming in and finding the two of you dressed like that. Or should I say undressed like that!'

His mouth hardened. 'My God, you'll use anything, won't you?' His eyes blazed and he stepped closer, rage making his face darker. 'Anything to hand, so long as it'll hurt!'

Lorel stared at him for a moment in silence, then shook her head and said fiercely, 'Go away, Steve! Just get out and shut the door and don't come back.'

She walked away to the window, looking out into the night, her glance flicking sideways, seeing that Katya and Max had gone, leaving the balcony quite deserted.

Turning, she looked back into her own darkened bedroom and saw Steve watching her, his hands deep in his robe pockets, his head lowered like an angry bull about to charge.

'Don't worry,' she said bitterly. 'I won't use it. There'll be no scandal. No pay-off. I just want to forget I ever knew you—any of you!'

He walked up behind her, bare feet soft on the polished wood floor. 'How can I be sure you'll keep your word?' he asked pointedly. 'Fleet Street could make you a very rich woman. It's a tempting way to make a fast buck.'

'Tempting for you, maybe!' she said, eyes spitting contempt. 'But I'd rather be able to look at myself first thing in the morning. Unlike you, I don't get enjoyment out of hurting other people, destroying their lives!'

His hands took her shoulders angrily and turned her to face him. 'Don't you?' he said tightly. 'Where's the proof of that?'

She jerked out of his grip. 'I don't need to prove myself to you!'

'You're not in the nursery now, darling!' he said under his breath. 'These are the Big Boys you're playing with. You'll find yourself fired if you don't give a guarantee of silence.'

She looked at him with dislike. 'What do you want me to do? Sign my name in blood?'

'You have to do something.' His eyes skimmed her face, scrutinising her as though he could read her thoughts and was confused by them. 'Max doesn't like his private life splashed all over the dailies. He can't take a scandal like this—it would kill him. He'd never get over it.'

Her eyes flashed. 'How kind of you to be *so* concerned about Max!'

'He's my friend!'

'He's your lover's husband!'

'Shut up!' he said thickly, his eyes black with rage. 'I can't take much more of that!'

'Oh, what a shame!' she purred, her own eyes dark with anger. 'Poor Steve! What's the matter—adultery too messy for you? Didn't you bargain on hurting her husband? On breaking up their marriage? Did you think it would be a jolly little affair with nobody hurt and nothing broken?' She could scarcely believe it was her talking; the words just tumbled out, vicious and deadly and aimed at his heart. She watched his face contort with rage as she aimed each poison-tipped arrow straight at him, saw him flinch, whiten, start to shake, and all the time she felt an answering pain in herself, a bitter and terrible regret that she was capable of doing this, hurting the man she loved just because he didn't love her.

'My God . . .' Steve said hoarsely, staring at her. 'How did I get involved with a woman like you? You're everything I hate!'

She flinched, eyes stinging: 'It works both ways! I didn't realise who I was dealing with when I fell for you! I thought you were a man I could——'

'What?' His hands clamped on her shoulder and he stared at her, eyes searching her face. 'Fell for me? What do you mean?'

The tears slid out hotly over her lashes. 'What's the point in lying to you?' She wrenched out of his grasp, closing her eyes tigtly as the tears slipped out. 'You must know already! Men like you always do. It's all calculated, isn't it? Make us fall in love with you and then move on to the next conquest. You don't even realise the damage you do. You play with love as though it were Monopoly, and the losers aren't supposed to care very much once the game is over.' Her eyes met his bitterly. 'But they do care, Steve! They care very much! And if I had any sense than I would sell my story to Fleet Street!'

He breathed erratically, watching her. 'Why are you saying that? Is it true? Or is it just another way of hitting back at me?'

'I heard what you said on the balcony, Steve!' Her eyes flashed with bitterness. 'That you were in love with me! How could you? How could you use me like that to cover up your affair with Katya? Don't you realise how much you hurt people when you——'

'Using you?' He stared at her. 'You're crazy! I've been in love with you for years!'

She looked away, sickened. 'Oh, please!'

'It's true!' His voice was a hoarse whisper. 'I fell hard and fast. I think it was when you were dancing. In the ballroom. You looked so wild, and I knew you were hurting like mad underneath all that bravado. I wanted to pick you up and wrap you in my arms so no one could ever hurt you like that again. You were drinking yourself into oblivion, dancing and flirting and dazzling.'

Her face burned. 'Don't remind me! I hated myself for the way I behaved!'

'Why?' His hand caught her chin, turned her to face him. 'You're human. You have a right to make a fool of yourself once in a while.'

Her laughter was bitter. 'I seem to do it every time I step outside my front door!'

'You were only eighteen, for God's sake,' he said. 'Can't you be a little more lenient on yourself?'

'That wouldn't be a good idea,' she said huskily. 'I'd only do it again.' Her eyes raised to his and she felt a stab of bitterness. 'I have done it again. With you. Look at what's happened . . .' her voice broke off and she turned her face away, holding back the tears.

He was silent for a moment, then said deeply, 'Lorel, I must know. Did you mean what you said? About falling in love with me?'

Silent, she tried to twist out of his grasp, her face white.

'Tell me!' His fingers tightened. 'You have to tell me. Is it true? Are you . . .' he paused, and his voice deepened as she said, 'in love with me?'

Her head lifted and she studied that arrogant face, the hard mouth and heavy-lidded eyes, the way his black lashes flicked gently on his cheekbones when he blinked, the thick black hair falling in freshly washed waves at his tanned forehead and strong neck. The way he held her. The way he looked at her. The sound of his voice.

'Yes.' Her eyes filled with tears and she nodded. 'Yes. I'm in love with you.'

There was a pause, then his arms were around her, holding her close, pressing her face against his shoulder, his breath escaping in a shuddering sigh from deep in his broad chest.

'I never forgot you. Not for one second through all those five years. You burned yourself into my memory in the space of six hours. I used to go over and over it in my mind, trying to figure out why you ran out like that. When I woke up that morning, I was devastated. I'd thought you'd stay. I'd pictured us having breakfast together, talking about the night before, going for a drive, going . . . I don't know. Just spending the day together. I couldn't believe you'd gone. Just left without a word.'

She kept her eyes closed, not daring to speak in case this turned out to be a dream in which she'd imagined everything, from the moment she woke up till the moment those strong arms went around her and made her feel she had come home at last.

'I was angry later. When I realised you weren't coming back, weren't going to get in touch with me. I waited the whole weekend. Drove past your house a few times. Sat outside. Watched you going out with your friends. Thought about going up and asking you what the hell you'd been playing at. But I couldn't find the nerve. I knew I had no right to expect anything from you. I knew you were infatuated with Robert.'

Lorel raised her head to stare at him. 'You did all

that . . . ?'

He looked at her. 'I didn't know what I was doing. I just kept going over and over that night in my mind. I cursed myself for being stupid enough not to make love to you. You sent me up in flames, I can remember holding you on that bed and almost dying for excitement.'

'And if you hadn't been in love with me?' she said huskily. 'What then? Would you have done it?'

'That's an irrelevant question. I wouldn't have caught you when you fell. I wouldn't have taken you to my room. None of it would have happened. It was a chain reaction. Not an isolated incident.'

'And this?' she asked softly. 'Is this a chain reaction, too?'

He was silent for a moment, then a lazy smile touched his mouth. 'What do you think?'

'I think it's very odd that you happened to have a flat just above mine,' she said, looking up at him through her lashes.

'Do you, now?' he drawled, eyes glittering. 'Well, you might just have a point there!'

She punched his shoulder, smiling. 'Tell me!

'No,' he drawled. 'I have to have *some* secrets.'

'Why?'

'Well—what would it do your ego if I told you I saw your name on the casting list for Eleanor, and immediately drove round to Larkswood Court to stake out the joint?'

She was touched. 'Did you do that?'

He studied her, the blue eyes flickering over her flushed face. 'As I said,' he drawled, 'I can see your head growing from here!'

Lorel could scarcely believe it. Obviously, he wasn't going to tell her the whole story—at least not for the moment. But it overwhelmed her as proof of his love, and she suddenly felt the chains that had bound her in mistrust and unhappiness start to fall away from her as though they had never existed.

'It's all so much simpler, isn't it?' she said huskily. 'To face things. I wish I'd stayed, that night. I wish I hadn't run away. But it was so awful when I woke up. It seemed so sordid.'

'Don't!' he said tightly. 'I knew you were thinking that and I hated you for it. Really hated you. You'd hit me like a runaway truck, darling. I was wide open and unable to defend myself. Knowing you must have been sickened when you woke up was too much for me to take. I'd never been kicked in the teeth quite so hard before.'

'Never?' Her eyes widened.

He made a face. 'Well . . . there was one rather chic little Frenchwoman when I lived in Paris. But that was twenty years ago. And it was a mere tap compared to——'

'Paris?' Her body turned to ice and she studied him. 'It was Katya—wasn't it? I heard you say you'd lived with her in Paris.'

He shook his head, smiling. 'Katya is a friend. Truly a friend. One of my oldest and most valued friends. But she is nothing more. I'm not in love with her——' He laughed, eyes dancing. 'It would be like falling in love with my sister! There's just no chemistry between us at all.'

Lorel tried to believe him, but after everything she had seen and heard over the last twenty-four house it was impossible, and she turned away, pulling out of the circle of his arms, standing a little way away from him, the wind lifting strands of her red-gold hair around her cool, pale face.

'I've seen you with her, Steve,' she said huskily. 'I know there's something between you.'

'This morning?' He shoved his hands in his robe pickets. 'At Gizeh? I was trying to make you jealous, Lorel. That's all.'

She shook her head, mouth tightening. 'Yesterday, Steve. I saw you in that bar with her yesterday as I drove in from the airport. The car stopped at a crossroads and I looked to the left. I saw you arguing. It looked likes a lovers' quarrel to me.'

'Oh, did it?' he drawled coolly. 'That just shows how good a judge of scenes you are!'

'Don't laugh at me!'

He face sobered. 'I was leaving for the airport last night when Katya ran out of the hotel, crying. She tried to hail a taxi, said she was leaving Max. I told her to wait, to come to the airport with me. I thought I could talk her out of it. I turned to hail a taxi for us, and when I looked back, she'd gone. Run off into the streets. It was crazy—I couldn't just let her go. She could have been killed.'

'So you went after her and asked Chris to meet me?' Lorel said stiffly.

His mouth hardened. 'It wasn't that simple. Chris was watching, he saw what happened. I grabbed hold of him and told him to go and meet you while I caught up with Katya. She lead me a merry chase—through every dangerous street in Cairo. When you saw us at the bar I'd only just caught up with her.'

Lorel shook her head, looking at him with pain-filled eyes. 'I saw you come back in the taxi. You kissed her.'

His eyes flashed. 'You kissed Robert! On the doorstep. Wearing your négligé after spending the night with him!'

She flushed hotly and turned away. 'That's different!'

'Why?' His hand bit into her shoulder and turned her to face him. 'Because it's you?'

'No!' she cried, but she knew he was right, she was being judgemental.

'I think it is, Lorel!' His mouth was tight. 'And I've known Katya a damned sight longer than you've known Robert.'

'Robert was under stress,' she said huskily. 'He needed me.'

'And Katya needs me,' he said flatly. 'Her husband is going through an appalling crisis. He's approaching old age fast and he can't handle it. He's terrified. He looks into his next decade and sees it taking him into retirement. Yet he's married to a beautiful young woman of thirty-eight.'

Lorel looked up at him through her lashes, wondering how that must feel. Max was an important man and a very attractive one, even if he was nearly sixty. Was it true that that was the real problem between Max and Katya?

'Every time she's with a man younger than himself, Max goes beserk,' Steve continued deeply. 'Really beserk. He's got a ferocious temper and he's given Katya hell these last two years. It just gets worse, not better. God knows what he'll be like on his sixtieth birthday. Sheer bloody hell, I should think.'

Lorel studied him. 'If she's afraid of arousing his temper, why does she spend so much time with you?'

'Oh, come on, Lorel.' He watched her and sighed, running a hand through his hair. 'Where do you turn when you're worried or unhappy?'

She was silent, studying him.

'A friend. You turn to a friend, don't you?' The blue eyes flickered over her face carefully. 'You turn to someone who knows both you and your husband equally well. Someone who can actually make you feel a little less frantic.'

'Katya doesn't look exactly frantic to me!' Lorel remembered the woman's cool insolence this morning when she had spoken to her, that perfect face almost made of porcelain, with her big blue eyes and cold mouth.

'She was France's best actress,' he said coolly. 'She gave it up years ago, but she still knows how to use it. Believe me.'

She turned away, not knowing what to believe any more. It all sounded so plausible. Particularly his speech about falling in love with her . . . oh, God, she wanted to believe that! She wanted to trust him, wanted to be able to put her arms around him, too. But how could she possibly, when everything pointed towards his being either the man she had always hoped he was—or the biggest skunk this side of the jungle?

'Lorel,' he said deeply, 'Katya loves Max. He's everything to her. She wouldn't jeopardise her marriage for an affair with a friend. And I don't think she'd jeopardise her friendship with me by trying to involve me in adultery. In fact, I know she wouldn't.'

'But she seems to have done so, doesn't she, Steve?' Her eyes met his and she raised her brows, 'Max believes it——'

'Max is jealous of every man who talks to her,' he said coolly. 'He has been since he turned fifty-five. He can't accept that she just isn't going to leave him. He looks at her and sees all that beauty. He looks at himself and he sees an old man.'

'A very attractive and wealthy old man,' Lorel pointed out carefully.

'Lorel,' Steve drawled lazily, 'her heart belongs to Daddy.'

Her lips parted and she said, 'Is that why she married him?'

'Of course!' He smiled, coming towards her and sliding a hand beneath her rich red hair. 'Hadn't you figured that out? I know she looks very cool and capable, but she just wants a big strong Daddy to look after her.' He laughed under his breath. 'The old clichés are the nicest!'

'Does he know?'

'He did at one stage,' he drawled, 'but he seems to have temporary amnesia. That's one reason why it's hitting Katya so hard. He isn't looking after her any more. She's lost. It's driving her out of her mind.'

Lorel looked away. 'Poor Katya . . .' Yes, she could see it now. If she closed her eyes and forget they were married, she could just about believe Katya and Max were an elegant father and daughter, both so well dressed, so impeccably mannered, so icy-cool. They were a couple of finely polished bookends, and at the moment they were standing tall and proud, back to back, refusing to look at each other.

How strange and complex human relationships are, she thought. Katya did seem cool and controlled, yet when Max had stepped into that room she had fallen to pieces, and struggled to retain her dignity in the face of the waves of disapproval and anger coming from her husband.

Thinking back, she could also remember how her face had been when she was talking to Steve. Warm and friendly, yes. But no passion. Not in her cool mouth and not in her perfect eyes. Not a trace of passion. Yet when Max entered the room she had come alive with it, her face etched and strained, her body tense as she watched her husband walk on to the balcony.

'Well?' Steve was watching her from beneath hooded lids. 'Do you believe me? Or do I have to take you next door and cause a massive scene with Katya and Max until I've got you convinced?'

She stared at him. 'I . . .'

'Hey,' he said, 'I need someone on my side in this. I'm getting it from all angles at the moment, and I need some support.'

She looked away, her mouth dry. 'It's such a gamble . . .'

'Yes,' he said in a heartfelt tone, 'it is. Anything worth having in life is a gamble. I can't guarantee that we won't argue or hate each other, or even end up strangling each other. But I can guarantee that I love you desperately . . .' His voice grew husky, and he added, 'Even if you are an obstinate little crosspatch who doesn't know a good thing when she sees it!'

Tears blurred her eyes and she blinked them back, irritated with herself for being moved so easily. 'You, I take it, are the good thing?'

He laughed. 'We're a fine bunch, we Kennedys!'

Lorel slid her arms around her neck, her cheeks dimpling. 'Modest, too.'

He was watching her seriously, and she sobered, her eyes meeting his in the sudden silence. She felt his heart thud an unsteady beat against her breasts, and she realised he was nervous.

'Then you're beside me?' he asked. 'All the way?'

She nodded, her face serious.

He smiled slowly. 'Thank God for that. For a minute there I thought I'd have to put you across my knee!'

Excitement flashed in her eyes and she couldn't help saying softly, 'Did you, sir?'

'Wow . . .' he said thickly, hands tightening on her waist as he pulled her towards him and murmured, 'Who does *your* heart belong to? Your friendly neighbourhood headmaster?'

Lorel moaned as his mouth found her throat and

nipped softly at her while her hands slid over his shoulders, holding him very close indeed. Her pulse-rate soared, and her lids closed as she abandoned herself to the demanding, hungry kiss that came a moment later when his hard mouth covered hers.

Freedom exhilarated her as she slid her hands under the neck of his robe, feeling the hot, tanned flesh smooth beneath her fingertips, heard him groan from the back of his throat, felt that hard mouth increase the pressure of hers as passion flared deeper between them.

'Hey . . .' he raised his head a moment later, breathing roughly, 'don't forget I'm naked under this . . .'

She looked up through gilt-tipped lashes. 'So am I . . .'

He studied her in silence, his jaw tight with desire, and the blue eyes burned hungrily on her lips, on the parting of her robe at her breasts. Then he closed his eyes and muttered something under his breath.

She went very still. 'What did you say?'

'I said,' he spoke as though it was dragged from his stomach, 'I'm not going to make love to you until we're married.'

'Married!' She caught her breath, staring. She could hear his heart beating beneath the white towelling robe, and saw a sudden flash of vulnerability in his blue eyes, his mouth held taut as he waited for her answer. She loved him. But would it work? Did he really love her enough to make it work? If only there was a guarantee for these things. If only she could see into the future. But that was impossible. He had said it already—the only surefire way to make it work was to hold her nose and jump in, trusting him completely. What would she want to see, though—if she could look into the future? A picture flashed into her mind of a cottage in the English countryside, Steve working by a sunlit window on a screenplay while she cooked lunch for a couple of dark-haired, blue-eyed children. Dogs, flowers in the window, a cheerful, disciplined nanny to look after her children when she felt that strong urge to move back into the world and work as an actress, before coming back after a while to tend her valley home again.

She didn't only need Steve. She needed an awful lot more than her man. She needed herself, and she needed children and a home. But if she had to pick just one from all the things she needed to make her happy, it would be Steve, because he was the only one ingredient that could keep her happy all by himself, whereas the others would be empty and painful to live for without him.

'That was a proposal, Lorel,' Steve said deeply. 'I'd like an answer.'

She lifted her face to his. 'Darling, I couldn't marry anyone else.' And as she said the words, she knew it was true. Had she fallen in love with him five years ago? Was that what had thrown her into emotional limbo for so long? She couldn't answer that yet. She only knew that she loved him now, and the mists of the last five years were clearing, leaving her hand in hand with Steve, facing the future together.

His eyes held hers and he said sincerely, 'I'm glad

you finally figured that out.'

'I think I've always known.'

'Odd, isn't it? My mother always said I'd know the girl I was going to marry the minute I set eyes on her.' He laughed. 'I hate my mother! She's always right!'

She laughed. 'I can't wait to meet her!'

'Oh, she'll love you!' he drawled. 'You'll be able to sit and agree with her about how selfish and bad-tempered and pig-headed I am.'

'How nice for me,' said Lorel, 'to have someone who will understand.'

The blue eyes glittered at her from beneath heavy lids. 'Insolent wench!' he said, baring his teeth, and bent his head to kiss her quite mercilessly until she clung to him, glad to know that he was the man she had always imagined herself standing at the altar with, someone tall and dark and very, very strong.

'I feel marvellous!' Steve said with a quick smile. 'Let's do something exciting! Let's go for a carriage ride along the Nile!'

He caught her and and pulled her towards the door.

'We're not dressed!' Lorel protested, laughing, and he turned, taking her blue button-through dress from the chair she'd left it on, handing it to her and turning his back while she wriggled into it, buttoning it up quickly.

Then they were out in the corridor, and Steve was taking the key from his robe, opening his door without thinking and flicking the light switch on.

'Oh!' He flushed and stood frozen in the doorway,

'Sorry! I'd completely forgotten you were here . . .'

Katya and Max were scarlet with mortification, standing up from the bed after a passionate embrace and running trembling hands through their hair, straightening their clothes.

Steve watched them for a moment, his face surprised. Then he relaxed, leaning lazily in the doorway. 'Do I take it Max has come to his senses?'

Max cleared his throat, quickly recovering his dignity. 'I feel I must apologise to you, Steven. My behaviour tonight was totally out of character. I can only offer the defence that I——'

'No need, Max.' Steve held up one long hand and smiled. 'No need.'

Max met his gaze and a look of silent affection passed between the two men that touched Lorel. She dropped her gaze, smiling.

Steve put one arm out, slid it around Lorel and pulled her gently into the picture. 'Tonight seems to be the night for all of us,' he said lazily. 'I just got engaged.'

Katya and Max stared for a moment, then they were stepping forward to congratulate, and Max was ringing room service for champagne to be sent up.

'Excuse me . . .' Steve murmured in Lorel's ear, and disappeared into the bathroom with a white shirt and denim jeans over one arm.

Lorel stared after him, feeling suddenly uncomfortable, as though she didn't belong to this tight-knit little group who had known each other for so long that they were almost a family.

'I've been rather unkind to you,' Katya said quietly,

watching her.

Lorel lifted her chin defensively. 'You were concerned for Steve,' she said, trying to appear as cool as the other woman. 'It's understandable.'

Katya smiled. 'I must apologise. Obviously there was a misunderstanding. There always is in love, isn't there?' She laughed. 'Men! What can we do about them?'

'I take it your problems are solved, too?' Lorel said uncertainly, her gaze flicking from one to the other.

Katya nodded. 'Our roller-coaster slipped off the tracks for a moment. But we always manage to get it back on.'

'I'm glad,' Lorel said quietly. 'I don't like the idea of divorce. It seems so painful and unnecessary.'

'Good. Then Steven has chosen well,' she said softly.

Steve came out of the bathroom, whistling and glancing in the mirror, running fingers through his hair. 'Ready?'

She nodded, laughing at his careless vanity.

He caught her hand. 'We're going to do something romantic,' he drawled, opening the door. 'Don't wait up for us!'

'But the champagne . . . !' Max began.

'I think you have something to celebrate, too, don't you?' Steve raised dark brows.

There was a short silence, then Max nodded, a smile touching his mouth.

Steve whirled Lorel out of the bedroom before

she could think, then they were riding down in the lift together, walking out into the noisy Cairo night that was fresh and alive and filled with excitement. Steve raced into the centre of the dusty street and hailed a carriage that clip-clopped up beside them with a toothless driver.

'Let's have a coach and four at the wedding,' Steve said as they got in. 'A white one with plumed horses.'

'Well, to be honest,' she said carefully, 'I've always wanted a 1920s Rolls-Royce. And a band playing the Charleston at the reception.'

'Oh, no!' He shook his head. 'It's got to be something with a bit more punch! Madonna. Or The Stones.'

'What?' She stared, aghast, as they clip-clopped alongside the starlit Nile, palm trees and moonlight all around them.

'I might consider a good jazz band!' Steve mused. 'We can knock them out on the dance-floor, then honeymoon in the Bahamas!'

Her eyes narrowed. 'Not the Bahamas!'

He bared his teeth. 'Don't argue!'

'How selfish can you get? Whose wedding is this?'

'Ours!' he said, laughing and sliding his arms around her. 'And I can see it's going to be a lively affair!'

'Particularly if you won't let me have my Rolls-Royce and my——'

'Save it for the wedding night,' he drawled, pressing his mouth over hers with burning passion.

'You're going to need all your enegry for that because, believe me, I'm going to spend at least five months making love to you if this keeps up . . .'

Harlequin Presents

Coming Next Month

1199 THE ALOHA BRIDE Emma Darcy
Robyn is at a low point in her life and is determined not to be hurt again Then she meets Julian Lassiter Somehow she finds herself wanting to solve Julian's problems in a way that is not only reckless but is positively dangerous!

1200 FANTASY LOVER Sally Heywood
Torrin Anthony's arrival in Merril's life is unwanted and upsetting, for this shallow, artificial actor reminds her of Azur—the heroic rebel sympathizer who'd rescued her from cross fire in the Middle East Could she possibly be mixing fantasy with reality?

1201 WITHOUT TRUST Penny Jordan
Lark Cummings, on trial for crimes she's innocent of, hasn't a chance when she is faced with James Wolfe's relentless prosecution Then the case is inexplicably dropped. She wants to hate this formidable man, but finds it impossible when fate brings him back into her life!

1202 DESPERATION Charlotte Lamb
Megan accepts a year apart from her newfound love, Devlin Hurst—she'll wait for him Yet when her life turns upside down just hours after his departure, she knows she must break their pact. Only she has to lie to do it

1203 TAKE AWAY THE PRIDE Emma Richmond
Toby lies about her qualifications to become secretary to powerful Marcus du Mann—and is a disaster But when Marcus gets stuck with his baby nephew, Toby is put in charge. And she's coping well—until Marcus decides to move in and help

1204 TOKYO TRYST Kay Thorpe
Two years ago, Alex walked out on Greg Wilde when she discovered he was unfaithful Now they're on the same work assignment in Japan. Despite Greg's obvious interest in the beautiful Yuki, Alex finds herself falling in love with him all over again!

1205 IMPULSIVE GAMBLE Lynn Turner
Free-lance journalist Abbie desperately wants a story on reclusive engineer-inventor Malacchi Garrett. Then she discovers the only way to get close to him is by living a lie. But how can she lie to the man she's falling in love with?

1206 NO GENTLE LOVING Sara Wood
Hostile suspicion from wealthy Dimitri Kastelli meets Helen in Crete, where she's come to find out about the mother she never knew What grudge could he hold against a long-dead peasant woman? And how would he react if he learned who Helen is?

Available in September wherever paperback books are sold, or through Harlequin Reader Service:

In the U.S.
901 Fuhrmann Blvd.
P.O. Box 1397
Buffalo, N.Y 14240-1397

In Canada
P.O. Box 603
Fort Erie, Ontario
L2A 5X3

ℋ*arlequin American Romance*®

Gull Cottage

The sun, the surf, the sand...

One relaxing month by the sea was all Zoe, Diana and Gracie ever expected from their four-week stay at Gull Cottage, the luxurious East Hampton mansion. They never thought that what they found at the beach would change their lives forever.

Join Zoe, Diana and Gracie for the summer of their lives. Don't miss the GULL COTTAGE trilogy in Harlequin American Romance: #301 CHARMED CIRCLE by Robin Francis (July 1989); #305 MOTHER KNOWS BEST by Barbara Bretton (August 1989); and #309 SAVING GRACE by Anne McAllister (September 1989).

GULL COTTAGE—because one month can be the start of forever...

GULLG-1